"You're trying to seduce me."

"Would I do that?" Brendan would, but Jo had turned the tables. The heat in her eyes stirred him up something fierce.

"You're angling for an invitation back to my place tonight."

"Are you considerin' it?"

"I explained earlier why that's a bad idea."

"I know, but—"

"I'm not considering it."

"Damn."

"Okay, maybe I did for a split second."

"Then let's keep dancin'. Lots of split seconds left in this number."

"Doesn't matter. I have my plan."

"You're a stubborn lady."

"And you're a stubborn man. Much to my surprise, I find that arousing."

"Me, too. You present a challenge. I do like a challenge."

A COWBOY'S CHOICE

THE MCGAVIN BROTHERS

Vicki Lewis Thompson

Ocean Dance Press

Want more cowboys? Check out these other titles by Vicki Lewis Thompson

The McGavin Brothers
A Cowboy's Strength
A Cowboy's Honor
A Cowboy's Return
A Cowboy's Heart
A Cowboy's Courage
A Cowboy's Christmas
A Cowboy's Kiss
A Cowboy's Luck
A Cowboy's Charm
A Cowboy's Challenge
A Cowboy's Baby
A Cowboy's Holiday
A Cowboy's Choice

Thunder Mountain Brotherhood
Midnight Thunder
Thunderstruck
Rolling Like Thunder
A Cowboy Under the Mistletoe
Cowboy All Night
Cowboy After Dark
Cowboy Untamed
Cowboy Unwrapped
In the Cowboy's Arms
Say Yes to the Cowboy
Do You Take This Cowboy?

Sons of Chance
Wanted!
Ambushed!

Claimed!
Should've Been a Cowboy
Cowboy Up
Cowboys Like Us
Long Road Home
Lead Me Home
Feels Like Home
I Cross My Heart
Wild at Heart
The Heart Won't Lie
Cowboys and Angels
Riding High
Riding Hard
Riding Home
A Last Chance Christmas

<u>**1**</u>

Brendan Sawyer strolled into the Eagles Nest Community Bank with his life savings in his pocket and hope in his heart. He'd cut his ties to Australia. No going back. Only forward.

Asking Jo Fielding to dinner was the first step in his journey. To say she held his future in her hands might be a bit dramatic, but a hell of a lot depended on her response. A trickle of sweat ran down his spine despite the blast of frigid air he brought in with him.

Jo wasn't in evidence. Good. Gave him a chance to catch his breath, get his bearings. When he'd visited during Christmas he'd had no reason to come into the historic brick building that housed the bank.

The sturdy oak counters and polished wood floor telegraphed stability, an excellent quality for a financial institution. The place was classy, like Jo. His money would be safe here.

The small lobby was empty and only one teller was on duty, a willowy blond. Her nametag identified her as Libby. She glanced up with a smile. "How may I help you?"

"Yes, ma'am." He tipped his hat. "I'd like to open an account. Checkin', savings and a few CDs."

Her smile widened. "I thought I recognized you. You're Quinn Sawyer's brother."

"Guilty as charged."

"I heard a rumor you might be moving here."

"Couldn't resist after that humdinger of a Christmas talent show."

"I know, right? If you'll have a seat in the lobby area, I'll see if Jo Fielding's back from lunch. She'll be the one to set up your accounts."

"Much obliged." He settled into one of two leather wingbacks positioned near the wall and stared at a large Remington print on the opposite wall. Showtime. He and Jo had flirted a bit during his Christmas visit, but that didn't mean she'd—

"Hello, Brendan."

He popped up and whisked off his hat as she walked toward him. "G'day, Jo."

"Welcome to Eagles Nest."

"Thanks. Guess you got the word I'd be comin' by."

She smiled like she was glad to see him. "Yep."

He smiled back. Damn, she looked good. Her moss-green sweater brought out the green in her eyes. He liked that she didn't color her hair, just let it turn gray like nature intended. She wore it super short, a wash-and-go style that went great with the silver hoop earrings she favored.

"Libby said you want to open an account with us."

"I do." He caught a whiff of her perfume, just enough to make his heart do a 'roo hop.

"Come on back and I'll get you set up."

He followed her down a short hall and through a doorway into a wood-paneled office that was right out of the eighteen-hundreds. Well, except for the computer monitor and keyboard on her antique oak desk.

"Have a seat." She gestured to the two oak chairs in front of her desk.

Taking his wallet out of his hip pocket, he waited for her to sit down before he did. "This is what I have to work with." He handed her a cashier's check.

Her eyes widened. Then she glanced at him. "Libby mentioned a savings account and some CDs, but I'd like to suggest a more sophisticated investment strategy."

"I was hopin' you would have some ideas." He propped his hat on his knee.

"I do, but first we'll need to discuss your long-term goals."

"I'm workin' on those, and I could use your help brainstormin'."

"I'd be happy to, although I have a two o'clock appointment that could run long. Tomorrow morning's fairly open, though. How about—"

"Or we could have a chat over dinner."

She blinked. "Dinner?"

"I think better with a beer in my hand."

"I see." She studied him for a moment. "Are you asking me out?"

"Yes, ma'am. Although I'm serious about the brainstormin'. Up to now I've just socked money away in an interest bearin' account, and I—"

"But in effect, this would be a date."

"Yea, yea, you could call it that." He shifted in his chair. "I was hopin' you'd be free tonight, since tomorrow's Valentine's. That night is...significant. Might not want to load a first date with a ton of significance." Enough was riding on it already.

"That's for sure." She toyed with one of her earrings as she gazed at him. Clearly she was thinking about the invite, which was better than a flat refusal. She stopped messing with her earring and folded her hands on the desk. "I'll meet you at six tonight at the Guzzling Grizzly, but just for a drink." Her tone didn't leave room for negotiation.

He flashed her a quick smile. "That'll do." It was a start.

"In the meantime, would you like me to deposit this in a basic checking account so you'll have access to it while you're choosing your course of action?"

"It'd be a relief. Never had this much money on me. Couldn't wait to turn it over to you."

"I understand." Her slender fingers danced over the computer keys as she took down his info.

Not much to it. He was staying at Quinn's place. His Social Security number was the same one he'd had since his first job in high school. He'd never applied for Australian citizenship. Never seriously considered it. Australia was amazing, but the USA was home.

She paused. "Do you want Quinn's address on the checks I order?"

"For now."

"Okay, that should take care of things for the time being." She handed him a small booklet of generic checks. "These should get you through until the printed ones arrive."

"Then I'll be off." He stood and put on his hat. "I could give you a lift to the GG tonight and show off my new truck."

"You already have a truck?"

"I will by tonight." He waved the thin checkbook. "Needed a bank account first. Want me to pick you up?"

"Thanks for the offer, but I'll stick with the plan and meet you there."

He grinned. "Evidently the thrill of ridin' in a brand-new truck isn't what it used to be."

"Oh, it still is." She met his gaze and smiled. "That's why I'll be driving myself."

* * *

Jo's last remark stuck with him all afternoon. Any way he looked at it, she'd basically admitted that he affected her. So much so that the combination of him and a snazzy truck might send her over the edge. That was tantalizing.

Choosing the truck was a blast. He considered a cozy two-door but a four-door expanded the possibilities for socializing. He insisted on heated seats. Just because he was tough didn't mean he didn't like being pampered.

Color was another tough call. He was drawn to badass black at first, but then a dark burgundy caught his eye. It had a top-of-the-line sound system and a moon roof.

He had a large dose of vehicle pride going on when he drove to the GG a few minutes before six. She hadn't arrived by the time he parked, so he chose a spot under a light. Luckily it had an empty space next to it. He got out and buttoned his coat.

Cold out here. Would've been smarter to stay in the truck or head inside, but damn it, he wanted her to admire his new truck. He checked his watch. Two minutes. He could handle that.

Turning up his collar, he leaned against the gleaming fender and crossed his arms. Jo pulled in about a minute later.

She was laughing as he opened her door and helped her out. "Didn't want me to miss it, did you?"

"Are you impressed?"

"Extremely." She pulled up the fur-trimmed hood on her black coat. "Love the color."

"I haven't locked it yet if you want to sit in it and breathe in the new truck smell." He gestured toward the passenger door.

"I'll bet I could breathe it in even better from the driver's seat."

"So you could." He followed her around to the other side and opened the door. "Lots of bells and whistles. Even more than I—"

"I love bells and whistles." She scooted in, rested her hands on the wheel and wiggled her tush. "Great seat."

"Heated."

"Awesome. I didn't get that option and now I wish I had."

Score. He couldn't wipe the silly grin off his face. This was turning out well. He fished the keys out of his pocket and handed them to her. "Switch on the power so you can hear the sound system. It rocks."

"Gotta have a good sound system." She turned the key and Kenny Chesney's *Everything's Gonna Be Alright* poured out of the speakers.

He'd take it as a sign. "Nice song."

"One of my favorites." She examined the dash. "This is laid out well. Easy to see. Wow, only forty-six miles on it."

"Hardly any of that is mine. Other folks test-drivin' it. I didn't have to go far before I knew this was the one."

She glanced down at him. "Have you taken Quinn and Kendra out in it?"

"Not yet. They went to Bozeman today and weren't back by the time I came over here."

"Kendra's going to drool over this baby." She stroked the dash.

The Chesney tune ended and Rascal Flatts came on with *Life Is a Highway.* He couldn't ask for a more appropriate tune. "Wanna take a spin? You can drive."

She glanced at him. "Are you sure?"

"I wouldn't let just anybody, but I'd let you." The song's catchy lyrics swirled around them.

She hesitated as Rascal Flatts serenaded them. "I'd have to move the seat."

"Grab that lever on the side. It's a power seat. Get it the way you want it. See how that feels."

A small motor whirred as she moved the seat up a few inches.

"How's that?"

"Good."

"Then buckle up. Take me for a ride." Closing the door, he jogged around to the passenger side and hopped in. "Start 'er up."

The dome light stayed on for a couple of seconds, revealing the excitement in her eyes as she looked at him. "This is a first. I've never driven someone else's truck when it had only forty-six miles on it."

"It's a first for me, too. I've never been a passenger in my own vehicle."

"Never?"

"No reason."

"But you have one, now?"

"Yes, ma'am."

"What?"

He laughed. "The same reason any man has for butterin' up a beautiful woman."

"Fair enough." She flipped back her hood and turned the key. "Let's go for a ride."

2

Jo blamed Rascal Flatts for going along with Brendan's plan. And the dazzling perfection of this beautiful truck. And his eagerness to share the excitement of buying it. When he'd walked into the bank today, the gleam in his gray eyes had confirmed that she was one of the reasons he'd left Australia.

Heady stuff, but she calmed herself long enough to back carefully out of the parking space. A fender bender would wreck the truck and the mood. She was digging the mood—flirtatious and daring.

After waiting for traffic to clear, she made a left, heading away from town instead of toward it. Into the night. "Handles great."

"Sure does. You warm enough?"

"Perfect."

"Excellent." Brendan settled back in his seat, hands resting lightly on his thighs, casual as can be. An old George Strait song followed Rascal Flatts, taking the tempo down a notch.

A clear, dry pavement rolled beneath the truck's hefty tires. Traffic was light on the two-lane. "I like this truck."

"Me too." He glanced over at her. "Ever owned one?"

"Nope. Always bought SUVs. But I like the height of this truck. Driving it is big fun."

"Glad you're enjoyin' yourself." He moved his seat all the way back and stretched out his legs. "Still not sure why you wouldn't let me buy you dinner, though."

"Because dating sucks."

"That's only because you've never dated me."

She snorted. "Evidently your ego's in fine shape."

"It was until you rejected my dinner invitation. I had to use this truck to prop it up again."

"Did that work?"

"Better'n I expected. You've fallen in love with it."

"I confess I have and it's partly the color. When I ordered the SUV, I debated between red and burgundy. I got the red, but if I had to choose today, I'd opt for the burgundy."

"Why's that?"

"It's darker, richer, with more depth to it. Like a robust wine."

"And robust sex."

She laughed. "I wondered if you'd jump on that opening." A shiver of awareness traveled up her spine.

"Couldn't resist. It's my favorite subject."

"And one we need to talk about." She'd never been this bold, but Brendan's arrival in town had inspired her. Time to shake things up.

"Hallelujah! A woman who doesn't play games. I've died and gone to heaven."

"That depends on what you think of my proposition."

"I love it."

"You haven't heard it yet."

"Don't need to. You had me at *proposition.*"

"Then here it is." Her blood hummed in her veins. "Let's skip the dating phase. It's inefficient and artificial. People put on their best clothes and their best manners, all the while hiding their real selves behind a veneer. Even if the people eventually sleep together, they—"

"I never climb into bed with my veneer on. It itches."

"I'm trying to make a point."

"And it's a valid one. Dating sucks. But it's the way things are done."

"Doesn't have to be."

"Oh?" He glanced at her. "Is this the part where we drive over to your condo and—"

"No."

"Damn."

"It's the part where I suggest we take a road trip and spend a long weekend together. After three days we'll know whether this works or not."

He sucked in a breath. "Wow."

"Am I moving too fast?"

"No, no. I'm all for it. Caught me by surprise, is all. I need a couple seconds to adjust my thinkin'. I didn't expect—"

"I know, but the timing is perfect. I get Monday off for President's Day, so we could leave Friday after the bank closes."

"You mean this weekend comin' up?"

"Strike while the iron is hot, as they say."

"God almighty, woman."

"You're freaking out."

"Not exactly. I just...could you pull over at the next wide spot?"

"Okay." She eased up on the gas pedal, checked her mirrors, and moved carefully off the road. A frozen ridge of snow crunched under the tires. "Want to drive?"

"No, you're doin' fine." He unsnapped his seatbelt. "We just need a different venue for this type of discussion. Leave the motor runnin' and the lights on. I'll come 'round to your side."

"What—" But he was out of the truck before she could finish her question.

Then he opened her door and glanced both ways before holding out his hand. "Coast is clear."

"Why are we getting out?" Might as well confirm her hunch.

"I'm hopin' you'll join me in the back seat."

Bingo. Her pulse rate shot up. "To make out?"

"Not necessarily, but it could happen. Might be time to give that a try since we're plannin' to head off on a lost weekend in two days."

"Um, guess so." She put her hand in his and stepped down. "It's not like I've visualized all the details of that plan."

"But you came up with a dynamite core concept." He guided her toward the rear of the truck and opened the door. "After you."

She was a little shaky as she scooted onto the back seat, partly from the cold but mostly from anticipation. She sat on the smooth leather seat and turned toward the door. "This is smart of you."

"It is?" He climbed in and shut the door.

"If we don't enjoy kissing each other, we can forget the weekend idea."

"No worries." He took off his hat and leaned forward so he could lay it on the front passenger seat. "We'll enjoy it."

"How can you be sure?"

"I just am." He turned back to her and his gaze held hers as he trailed his forefinger down the curve of her cheek.

"Okay." Her heart thumped fast and hard, leaving her breathless.

"You're sure, too, or you wouldn't suggest spendin' three days with me." Heat smoldered in his gray eyes. "Kissing you tonight isn't a test."

She swallowed. "Then what is it?"

Cupping her cheek in one hand, he leaned closer. "Let's call it a beginnin'." His lips brushed lazily over hers...once, twice....

Warm breath. Peppermint. Then he settled in with a sigh of pleasure and began to explore. The subtle movement of his mouth sent heat spiraling to her core. When his tongue began to work its magic, she trembled and clutched his shoulders.

So tender, the gentle pressure of his kiss, and yet...a soft groan telegraphed urgent needs tightly leashed. A thrill of awareness shot through her, lighting fires in intimate places. More. More of this.

He shifted the angle and took the kiss deeper. Leaning into him, she slid one hand up the back of his neck and buried her fingers in his thick hair. Then she began a passionate assault of her own.

He tasted of desire, pleasure, reckless abandon. She couldn't get enough of his sinfully sensual mouth, didn't want this kiss to ever—

A sharp rap on the window shattered the moment and she pulled back, gasping.

A flashlight on high beam illuminated the interior of the cab. "Everything okay in there?"

Brendan muttered something earthy and slightly scandalous. Then he swiveled on the seat and shielded Jo from view before buzzing down the window. "Evenin', officer."

"Same to you folks. Noticed you'd pulled off the road and wondered if you needed assistance."

Jo sat up straight and peered over Brendan's shoulder at one of her daughter's former classmates. "We're fine, Jeffrey. But thanks for checking."

"Mrs. Fielding? What are you doing...I mean, why are you—"

"I'd like you to meet Brendan Sawyer, Quinn's brother."

"Oh. Pleased to meet you, Mr. Sawyer."

"Likewise." Brendan didn't sound particularly pleased as he stuck his hand through the window for the obligatory handshake.

"Brendan and I are having a deep discussion. Solving the world's problems."

"Ah. I see."

"I'll bet you've had similar deep discussions out on this road."

"Uh, yes, ma'am, but not usually in the middle of February. Although I guess tomorrow is Valentine's Day. I'll leave you to your discussion, then. Say hello to Mandy for me."

"I will. Thanks, Jeffrey."

"No problem, Mrs. Fielding." He switched off the flashlight and returned to his patrol car.

Brendan rolled up the window. Then he started to laugh. "Shades of my misspent youth! I haven't been busted for makin' out in a parked car since high school."

"Me, either."

He turned to her. "How many times?"

"Just once. I was mortified and refused to park in the boonies after that. How about you?"

"Aw, geez, I don't know. A bunch. So this Jeffrey dude knows your daughter?"

"They went to school together. He came over to the house several times to get help with his geometry homework."

"Just our luck."

"It wouldn't have mattered which deputy happened along. I know them all."

"Small town. I should have figured on that. Are you mortified?"

"No. I think it's funny."

"Good. But our weekend getaway makes even more sense after this episode. I didn't totally comprehend the issues." He paused. "We could try to pick up where we left off, but—"

"The mood's shot to hell."

"Pretty much."

"And some other good Samaritan might show up. It's the shiny new truck that's the problem. Kids looking for a make-out spot don't drive a fancy rig like this, so anyone who sees it parked here thinks we have a problem."

"Tactical error on my part. Are you hungry?"

"Starving."

"Me, too. Can I buy you dinner, after all?"

"Well, I—"

"Don't call it a date. Call it a planning session. We still have to work out the details of this weekend and we both need to eat."

"When you're right, you're right. Who's driving?"

"You are. I enjoy watching you handle my truck. Turns me on."

"Turns me on, too."

"There you go. Win-win." He reached for the door handle but abruptly swung back to her. "One more for the road." Taking her by the shoulders, he pulled her close and captured her mouth.

No gentle brush of lips. This time he brought the heat. And she went up in flames. The firm thrust of his tongue sent warm rivers of desire flowing through her, melting her inhibitions, fueling her fantasies. She moaned and clutched the lapels of his coat, tugging him closer.

He deepened the kiss and undid the top button of her coat. Paused at the second button. Lifting his mouth a fraction away from hers, he gulped for air. "If I don't stop…clothes are comin' off. And we…could have…visitors…again."

"Uh, huh."

"So I'm stoppin'." With a heavy sigh, he released her. "Don't want you to be mortified."

"Thanks." She struggled for breath. "I like to think…I would have stopped you."

"Yea, you probably would have, but—"

"Don't count on it."

His soft chuckle in the darkened interior of the cab hinted at delicious intimacies to come. "That's what I like to hear."

<u>*3*</u>

"Do you think your cop friend will spread the word?" Brendan fastened his seat belt as Jo put the truck in gear and executed a U-turn.

"Jeffrey's a kind person and he likes me. My guess is he won't say anything, but if he does and word gets around, that's okay."

"You're sure?"

"If I worried about gossip, I wouldn't have invited you to go away for the weekend. Everyone we care about will know what we're up to."

"In general. But at least we won't be doing it under their noses."

"Exactly."

Choosing a spot on a country road outside town had been a mistake. Good thing he'd taught himself sexual restraint over the years. In his twenties, he would have barreled ahead when a woman kissed him the way Jo had a few minutes ago.

They'd be naked now instead of heading back to the Guzzling Grizzly for dinner. In preparation for that, she'd repaired her lipstick and he'd checked in the visor mirror to make sure he wasn't wearing any.

Thank God she had a plan that would take them out of the public eye. "Do you have a place picked out?" Might be tough getting reservations on the weekend after Valentine's Day. Not that he cared where they ended up. He'd just had a preview of how things would go once they were truly alone. He'd be happy with a cheap sleep in the middle of nowhere.

"That's the other part that seems made to order. A customer I've had for years reserved a resort getaway to surprise her husband. Meanwhile he booked a trip to Hawaii to surprise her. He told her this morning. The resort has a no-refund policy because it's a Valentine's weekend special price and so she transferred the reservation to me."

"Would you have gone by yourself?"

"Yep. It was either that or give it away, although all the couples I know have already made plans for the weekend. Then you showed up and I thought *why not*?"

"Glad I can help." A resort. Room service. Champagne in an ice bucket. A king bed with luxurious sheets. Might even be a Jacuzzi in the deal. If he messed this up, he didn't deserve to win her heart. "Since you're lettin' me tag along, I'll cover gas and meals."

"Can we take your truck?"

"Want to?"

She laughed. "Duh. Like you said, I've fallen in love with it. The perfect choice for a new adventure."

"Then by all means, let's take it. Where is this resort?"

"West of here, near Anaconda. Just opened, which is why they're doing promotions. It's a little over two hours away."

Two hours to paradise. "How soon can we leave on Friday?"

"Excited, are you?"

"That's puttin' it mildly."

"Me, too. I've never done anything this…"

"Wild and crazy?"

"I was going to say that, but instead it's the opposite of wild and crazy. I can't think of a more sensible way to handle a new relationship."

"Works for me." Sensible? Nah. Awesome? *Oh, yeah*. He was happier than a wallaby in a blackberry patch.

"It's way better than the torturous exercise called dating. Ugh." She blew out a breath. "And look at that! Here we are at the GG on what is officially *not* a date." She swung the truck into the parking lot. "Somebody took your spot."

"There's one over there." He pointed to the other side of the lot. "Two spaces, in fact."

"That's good. Less chance of it getting scratched up."

"This is a truck. It'll get scratched up. No worries if you ding it."

"Nice speech. I'll remind you of it the first time it happens."

"I'll take it in stride."

"Sure you will." She pulled in slowly, leaving enough space to keep from banging the driver's door against the pickup next to them.

"Good job."

"Thanks." She turned off the motor. "Listen, since this isn't a date, how about if we go Dutch?"

"No, ma'am."

She turned to him. "Why not?"

"Because I invited you. And you accepted, which means you're willin' to let me pay for your food. But I have to ask one thing about this non-date dinner."

"Okay."

"What happens after?"

"Nothing."

"Nothin'?" He gazed at her. "You sucked on my tongue."

"I know, but if you come over after dinner, we're into the awkward dating scenario I'm trying to avoid."

"How can we be if it isn't a date?"

"If you follow me home, it becomes a date. We'll have sex and—"

"Good sex."

"Okay, but then you'll have to—"

"*Really* good sex."

"And then you'll have to either leave or spend the night."

"You'll be wantin' me to spend the night."

"There, see? We'll face the whole morning-after awkwardness."

"Might as well get that out of the way. Then we won't have to deal with it on Saturday mornin'. We'll be in the groove."

"That's the whole point. We won't have awkwardness on Saturday morning. We eliminate the issue."

"How?"

"Think about it. We'll be in a neutral zone that's not mine or yours. We'll both have our stuff, like toothbrushes and clean undies. No work to go to or chores to do."

"Let me get this straight. Are you sayin' I won't be seein' you tomorrow or tomorrow night, either?"

"That's right. For the reason I just mentioned and also because it's Valentine's Day. Like you said earlier, it's loaded with significance."

He took a deep breath. "When I said that, I hadn't kissed you, yet. Now I want to do somethin' for Valentine's Day. It'll feel weird to ignore it completely."

"It'll also feel weird to make a big deal out of it. We're in the baby stages of getting to know each other."

"Maybe so, but—"

"Well, look who's here. Quinn and Kendra just parked beside us."

"Did they, now?" He loved his brother and admired Kendra, but the timing sucked. He turned around and waved at them. "How do you want to play this?"

"Only one way, in my opinion. We share a table with them."

He faced her again. "And announce our weekend plans?"

"Yep. I have two people I need to tell and she's one of them. I'll call Mandy after I get home tonight."

"I only have one person I have to tell and he's climbin' out of his truck even as we speak. You're probably right. Go with the flow."

"They'll be cool with it. More so than my daughter, if I had to take a guess. They'll understand my reasoning. Mandy might not."

"What if they're meeting somebody here?"

"I hadn't thought of that, but I'd be amazed if they didn't invite us to join them, regardless."

"Alrighty, then. Full steam ahead." He reached for the door handle. "Should be an interestin' dinner." Getting out of the truck put him face-to-face with his brother.

Eyebrows lifted, Quinn surveyed the truck. "Nice ride. "

"It'll do. Jo likes it."

"That's good." Quinn looked like he wanted to bust out laughing.

"Oh, my God, Brendan!" Kendra, bundled up in a sheepskin coat and red knit hat pulled over her dark hair, rounded the tailgate of Quinn's truck. "It's gorgeous!"

"Isn't it?" Jo came from the other side of his truck and gave Kendra a quick hug. "I can't believe he let me drive it."

"Oh, I can." Quinn managed to keep his amusement confined, but his lips twitched with the effort.

Kendra glanced at Jo. "Are you guys here for dinner?"

"We are." Jo tugged her hood into place. "It was supposed to be just drinks but—"

"I sent you a text as we were leaving the house to see if you wanted to join us. Mandy was going to contact you, too."

"She's coming?" Jo fastened the top button of her coat, the one he'd undone.

"She and Zane are already in there. She had a sudden craving for Irish stew. You know how pregnant ladies get when they have a craving."

"Uh-huh. For me it was French fries."

"She texted me a few minutes ago and said she hadn't heard from you."

"Road noise must have blocked the sound of my phone."

"I guess you didn't hear yours, either, little brother." Quinn glanced at him.

"You called me?"

"Sent you a text. Figured you might want to join us since we don't have much in the fridge at home."

"And look at that. I ended up here anyway." He glanced at Kendra and Jo. "What do you say we all mosey inside where it's warmer?"

Kendra shivered. "Brilliant suggestion. It's freezing out here. Come on, Jo. Let's go see what our kids are up to."

The women walked ahead and Brendan fell into step beside his brother. "I would have offered you the first ride in my truck, but you weren't home."

"We were on our way back when we got the message from Zane and Mandy that they were heading over here." Quinn lowered his voice. "Just so you know, you have lipstick on your coat collar."

"Bugger. Which side?"

"The one nearest me. If you don't want the kids to see it—"

"I'd rather they didn't."

"Figured that. What if I suggest we all check our coats?"

"There's a coat-check option?"

"It's recent. Not everyone uses it, but I'm in the habit, now."

"Then let's do it. And just to give you a heads-up, Jo invited me to go away for the weekend."

"No shit."

"She was planning to tell you guys at dinner, but with Mandy here, she might hold off."

"Which weekend?"

"This one comin' up."

"I'll be damned. That must have been some make-out session."

"She invited me before that."

"*Really.*"

"She has a new strategy for handling relationships and she wants to test it out."

"What is it?"

"Better let her explain. We're runnin' out of real estate, especially if one of us intends to get the door for the ladies."

"I have to hand it to you, little brother. You've been here less than a week and you're already shaking things up."

He laughed. "I guess you've forgotten."

"Forgotten what?"

"It's what I do."

4

Jo talked fast as she and Kendra walked toward the GG's entrance. By the time Brendan opened the door for them, Kendra was up to speed on the weekend plan. And on board, thank God. She'd be a valuable ally in case Mandy didn't react well to the idea.

No telling how she'd respond. Following her parents' messy divorce, she'd escaped to New York for several years. She'd made brief visits home but hadn't asked if Jo was dating.

Jo hadn't volunteered the info, either, maybe because dating hadn't been much fun and Mr. Right hadn't shown up. She hadn't gone out with anyone since Mandy's return to Eagles Nest. This would be new territory for them.

When everyone was inside, Quinn took charge of their coats. If he hadn't suggested using the coat-check system, she would have. No need for Mandy to notice lipstick on Brendan's collar.

The GG was packed, unusual for a Wednesday night. A country band played and dancers two-stepped around the small dance floor.

Jenny, who'd worked at the GG for years, bustled over. "Welcome, welcome. I gave Mandy and Zane one of the round tables since they were hoping all of you would make it. That meant putting you guys more toward the back of the room."

"That's okay," Kendra said. "It's easier to talk when you're not so close to the band."

"That's true. Is Quinn here?"

"He's taking care of our coats." Jo located Mandy sitting with Zane and waved. They waved back and smiled. In a fairy-tale ending, her tow-headed daughter had married Kendra's raven-haired son and now they were expecting a child.

Life was following a lovely, uncomplicated trajectory and she was about to change the dynamic. Her stomach flip-flopped as she turned back to Jenny. "The place is jumping tonight."

"We decided to make this Valentine's Week instead of confining it to one day."

"I hadn't heard that." Jo glanced at Brendan. "Had you?"

"No, ma'am. Sure is festive lookin', though."

"Sure is." Vases of red and white chrysanthemums sat on every table. The usual gingham tablecloths had been replaced with white lace and red napkins. Giant foil hearts hung from the rafters and cupid cutouts decorated the walls. Evidently she'd share a valentine-themed meal with Brendan, after all.

After Quinn arrived they moved in single file back to the table.

Zane got to his feet. "Hey, Aunt Jo and Uncle Brendan. Our texts must have finally made it through."

Aunt Jo and Uncle Brendan? She was used to being called Aunt Jo. Kendra had assigned her the honorary title when their kids were little. Brendan's honorary uncle status was recent, though, and pairing him with her was unnerving, especially under the circumstances.

Mandy beamed at her. "I knew you'd be here, Mom. You don't go long without checking your messages. Especially now."

"Right."

"I ordered the cutest crib mobile today. If you sit by me, I can show you on my phone."

"Okay." Broaching the subject of a weekend with Brendan was gonna be tricky. Even though he'd followed her around the table, pulled out her chair and sat next to her, Mandy was oblivious.

"Here it is." She held out her phone. "Is that perfect or what?"

"Absolutely." The mobile consisted of several colorful birds in flight. "Guaranteed that baby will be a birdwatcher from the get-go."

"A birdwatcher and a horse whisperer." Kendra sat beside Zane. "I can't wait for this blessed event, although I'm thrilled that you're having this kid in July. Cody and Faith's December baby posed some challenges."

"Aw, it was fun." Quinn took the remaining chair between Kendra and Brendan. "Memorable."

"Wish I'd been there." Brendan's knee touched Jo's under the table. Likely no accident. "Carolin' outside their A-frame to welcome little Noel...you'll have to go some to beat that next time."

"We won't be caroling," Kendra said. "Or freezing our hineys off, thank heavens."

"I've been wondering what you'll come up with." Zane glanced at his mom. "Any hints?"

"No way. But rest assured that Granny Jo, Grandpa Quinn and I will create a fitting welcome for the little tyke."

Brendan rested his forearms on the table. "I notice nobody's sayin' whether it'll be a boy or a girl."

"We're not, Uncle Brendan." Mandy put down her menu and leaned around Jo. "Not knowing until the birth was so much fun for Cody and Faith that we decided to do the same."

He nodded. "Surprises are fun."

What a perfect segue to an announcement about the weekend getaway. She took a deep breath. "Speaking of surprises, I—"

"Ready to order?" Jenny appeared, digital notepad in hand.

Shoot. Now she'd have to work up to it again. "A glass of your Outrageous Red, please."

"Make that two," Kendra said. "No, wait. Let's you and me share a bottle."

"I can't drink half of it. I'm driving."

"No worries." Brendan gave her a quick glance. "I'll take you home."

She almost laughed at his eager comment. She'd just bet he would take her home. He still didn't share her conviction that they'd be happier if they waited until they were alone in a luxury hotel room before they had sex.

Didn't matter whether he subscribed to the concept or not. She was sticking to it. "Thanks, but—"

"Let's get the bottle," Kendra said. "We might decide to stay and dance."

Quinn nodded. "We very well might."

"A bottle it is, then." Jenny took the rest of the drink orders—beer for the guys and hot herbal tea for Mandy—and left.

"Speaking of dancing." Quinn looked over at his brother. "I haven't seen you out on the floor in years. Do you remember how?"

"Are you kiddin'? I was born dancin'. Picked up some new moves Down Under, too."

"This I gotta see."

Brendan glanced at her. "You up for a little dancin'?"

"I'm in." She was a card-carrying member of the Whine and Cheese Club, after all. Gave her a chance to find out if she and Brendan danced well together.

"I'm in, too," Mandy said. "But I might not be able to stick around as long as you guys. I'm an early-to-bed girl these days."

"I'm in if you're in." Zane looped an arm over her chair. "At least until you conk out."

Jenny returned with a loaded tray, passed out drinks and opened the wine. "Is everyone ready to order?"

"I'm so ready," Kendra said.

"You've got it." Jenny poured wine for Kendra and Jo and took orders from everyone before hurrying back to the kitchen.

Now or never. Jo took a gulp of wine and cleared her throat. "Before we hit the dance floor, I wanted to mention something. This morning one of my long-time customers gave me a reservation she's not able to use. It's for this weekend at a resort over by Anaconda and I've decided to go."

Mandy's eyes widened. "You're leaving town?"

"Just Friday afternoon through Monday afternoon. I'll have my cell phone if you—"

"Oh, hey." Mandy flapped her hands in the air. "Ignore my knee-jerk reaction. Blame the hormones. I'll be fine."

"You're allowed to be a little needy when you're preggers," Kendra said. "I'm right next door if a problem crops up."

Zane smiled and gave Mandy a little nudge with his shoulder. "And I'm right in the same house."

"There, you see, Mom? I'm loaded with backup and it'll be a nice break for you. Have you found somebody to go with? Sounds like the kind of thing that would be more fun with two people."

"I have found someone to go with."

"That's great! Who?"

"Brendan."

Mandy's eyes grew wide and her mouth dropped open. Then she turned toward Kendra and Quinn. "You're not surprised?"

"We met your mom and Brendan out in the parking lot," Kendra said. "They filled us in a little bit."

"Don't you think it's…suddcn?"

Kendra shrugged. "Depends on your perspective."

"But they hardly know each other."

"I know him well enough." Jo held back a smile. "He's not just some guy. He's Quinn's brother and I'm…attracted to him."

"I noticed that at Christmas, but he wasn't here long. And he just got back a few days ago. I wondered if you guys might start dating, but I never expected—"

"I hate dating."

"Is that why you've never done it?"

"I have done it."

"Since the divorce?"

"Yes."

"How come I didn't know that?"

"You were living in New York and I didn't find anybody I liked well enough to mention it. The point is, I find dating a torturous process that takes forever. I want to cut to the chase."

Mandy blinked. "Whaaat?"

"You've dated. You know the issues. Why not condense the discovery period to three days instead of three months?"

"I…um…because it's…."

"I realize I've startled you. But it literally just came together today. Shari offered me the weekend trip this morning and Brendan asked me out on a date this afternoon. I suggested this instead. I think it's logical." Although logic had never caused her heart to race like this. Announcing her intentions out loud to her nearest and dearest was intense. And liberating.

"Makes perfect sense to me," Kendra said. "Quinn and I didn't date, either. He needed to repair his motorcycle, I invited him to stay at the ranch, and voila."

Mandy gazed at her. "That's not the same as heading off for the weekend."

"Maybe not exactly," Quinn said. "But it threw us together for several days so we could get to know each other as we really are. With dating, you get dressed up for it. You're always on. I agree with Jo. It's artificial."

Zane leaned forward and looked at Mandy. "We didn't date, either."

"Because we didn't need to. We grew up together."

"Which makes my point." Jo took a restorative sip of her wine. "You had that advantage, but Kendra and Quinn didn't. Brendan and I don't."

"And they're at a different stage of life than we are." Zane laid a hand on Mandy's arm. "They don't have time to waste. They—"

"Hold up there, son." Kendra gave him a pointed look. "I know you're only trying to help, but please derail that train of thought."

He frowned. "But isn't that why Aunt Jo wants to speed things up?"

"It sort of is," Jo said.

"But he's making it sound like you and Brendan have one foot in the grave."

"Which they clearly don't." Mandy turned toward her. "It just feels like you're rushing into this, Mom. That's not you. You always give yourself time to consider things carefully."

"I did consider this carefully. After Brendan left the bank this afternoon, I assessed the situation. I've been given a free weekend getaway and an interesting man is available to share it with me. It's a no-brainer."

"I'm not so sure."

"Of course you're not. You and I have never been in this situation."

"Mom and I have," Zane said. "It's weird when your mom gets interested in a guy."

"And on top of that," Quinn said, "I was staying at the ranch. At least your mom and Brendan are leaving town."

Mandy was quiet for a moment. "You're right. That's a plus."

"For me, too." Jo put her arm around Mandy's shoulders and gave her a hug. Throughout the exchange, Brendan hadn't said a word. Very wise of him. If he understood when to speak and when to be silent, that was a good beginning.

<u>5</u>

Brendan didn't have kids, but to his untrained eye, Jo had ninja parenting skills. The subject of their weekend getaway had been neatly handled. The appetizers arrived soon afterward so everyone decided to postpone the dancing until after the meal.

Mandy was more subdued than she had been before the big announcement, though. He resisted the urge to try and get on her good side. He wouldn't build up trust in one evening at the GG.

Toward the end of the meal, Michael Murphy, his niece Roxanne's husband and co-owner of the GG, came by to ask if everyone was satisfied with the food and the service. Brendan joined in the chorus of rave reviews.

Michael smiled and gave them a tip of his black Stetson. "Glad to hear it."

"We say the same thing every time you ask," Jo said. "Must get boring."

"Never. Besides, I didn't come over here to bask in your praise. I'm counting on my family to tell me the truth if anything's not right. Don't hold back."

"In that case..." Quinn picked up the cloth napkin from his lap, pulled reading glasses out of his pocket and inspected it. "The fold is about an eighth of an inch off center."

"Do tell."

"That's nothin' compared to the cattywampus placement of our bouquet." Brendan gestured to it. "No way that's in the middle of the table, mate."

Michael grinned. "Let me correct that for you, Uncle Brendan." He moved the vase about an inch.

"We're also short a flower," Jo said. "We only have three in our bouquet and those folks have four." She pointed to the next table over.

"And they have a square vase." Kendra picked up the round one. "I much prefer a square."

"I have the perfect solution. Be right back." Laughing, Michael grabbed the vase and left.

Zane rolled his eyes. "I hope you folks know what you just started. No telling what he'll...oh, God, here he comes."

Michael wound his way through the tables carrying a ginormous Valentine's bouquet. Had to be at least two dozen roses in it, half deep red and half snowy white. Sure enough, they were tucked into a large square glass vase.

He set it in the exact middle of the table. "How's that?"

Quinn smiled. "It'll do."

Brendan stared at the bouquet. "How in the devil did you come up with it so fast?"

"My secret."

"It's gorgeous, square vase and all," Kendra said. "But don't leave it here."

"I won't. I just wanted to show it off and you gave me the perfect excuse. I hope she'll like it."

"She'll love it, son." Quinn beamed at him. "Nicely done."

Then the bouquet was for Roxanne. Nice gesture. His niece had clearly married a true romantic.

"She will love it." Jo smoothed a finger over one of the rose petals. "Smells wonderful, too."

Aha. Jo liked roses. "Is there a florist in town?"

Michael shook his head. "I had to plan this way ahead. A florist in Bozeman agreed to have them shipped in and then deliver the bouquet to the GG so I could surprise Roxanne with it tonight."

"I take it she's not here, then."

"She's at home finishing a graphic design project. If she gets it done, that frees up some time so we can be together tomorrow." He lifted the bouquet. "I'll bring back the other one."

"No need," Quinn said. "We'll be burning up the dance floor instead of sitting at the table counting flowers in the vase."

Michael smiled. "I'll bring it anyway. Have fun."

"Thanks. We always do."

Kendra watched him weave through the tables carrying the vase. "That's a Valentine's Day meme right there—a broad-shouldered cowboy clutching a huge bouquet of roses. Young love is so sweet."

"Old love's not so bad, either." Quinn pushed back his chair. "Care for a dance, Granny Ken? We can show my little brother how it's done."

"Them's fightin' words, mate." Brendan stood and held out his hand. "Jo?"

She laughed and put her hand in his. "Is this a competition?"

"Damn straight. Are you with me?"

"You bet. I was born dancing, too."

"Then we're about to have one hell of a good time." He led her out to the floor. Dancing was a passion of his and if Jo shared his enthusiasm, what a bonus.

One glance at her animated expression and he had his answer. As he employed his favorite two-step moves, she was a responsive partner, limber as a willow in the wind.

Meanwhile Quinn and Kendra put on quite a show, too. In the old days, when the Sawyer brothers had been two young bucks out to prove something, they'd regularly cleared the dance floor. Evidently they still had that effect.

Ringed by a clapping, whistling crowd, he was in his element. Even better, Jo seemed to be, too. She matched his every move and anticipated the next. As the band swung into the final few bars of the tune, he spun her around the perimeter in a blistering triple-step, twirling her under his arm and behind his back.

One final spin and it was over. He faced her, breathless and grinning. "Awesome."

She gulped for air. "Sure was. I've never danced the two-step that fast. I'm ready to sit dow—"

"Hang on a sec. The band's playin' a cool-down number. It's better for our systems if we don't sit just yet."

"You're making that up." But she didn't resist when he drew her into his arms.

"I'm not makin' it up. Goes for any strenuous physical exercise. Your body needs to gradually return to a restin' phase. You don't want your muscles crampin', do you?" He tugged her in closer.

"They won't." She nestled against him. "I do yoga and get regular massages."

"In other words, you take care of yourself."

"I do."

"I can tell." First time he'd had full-length contact with her lithe, toned body. Nice. Maybe a little too nice. His buddy was responding to that gentle friction.

Her boots gave her extra height and she only had to tilt her chin slightly to meet his gaze. Her mouth was within kissing distance. "Are you sure this is supposed to cool us down?"

"Um...I might have miscalculated on that score."

"I don't believe that for a minute." Her hips moved in sync with his. "You're trying to seduce me."

"Would I do that?" He would, but she'd turned the tables. The heat in her eyes stirred him up something fierce.

"You're angling for an invitation back to my place tonight."

"Are you considerin' it?"

"I explained earlier why that's a bad idea."

"I know, but—"

"I'm not considering it."

"Damn."

"Okay, maybe I did for a split second."

"Then let's keep dancin'. Lots of split seconds left in this number."

"Doesn't matter. I have my plan."

"You're a stubborn lady."

"And you're a stubborn man. Much to my surprise, I find that arousing."

"Me, too. You present a challenge. I do like a challenge."

"About that." She wound her arms around his neck and swayed with the music. "I saw your expression when Michael brought out Roxanne's bouquet. I'm warning you—do *not* get me roses and have them delivered to the bank. I'm not your valentine."

"Couldn't swing it, anyway. Not enough time to get primo roses." Her hips tucked against his package had created a predictable problem. He should put some distance between them since he couldn't return to the table in this condition. But he didn't want distance. He wanted what she'd informed him he couldn't have tonight.

"I realize you couldn't come up with a bouquet like that on short notice, but please, I'm asking you, don't turn yourself inside out looking for a substitute gift."

"Under the circumstances, ignorin' the day seems wrong."

She studied him. "Are you really that much of a romantic?"

"This time of year I am. Valentine's Day is a big deal in 'stralia. Even if you're casually datin' someone, that day is significant."

"All we've done so far is kiss."

"I put my tongue in your mouth. In some cultures, your relatives would be loadin' a shotgun."

She sighed. "Promise me you won't make any Valentine's Day gestures. It's not appropriate."

"Okay, I promise, but let the record show that I don't like it. We shared a hot kiss, two in fact, and we're goin' away for the weekend. If that's not a valentine scenario, I don't know what is."

Keeping time to the music, she cupped his face in her soft, warm hands. "Just because you have a strong sexual attraction to me doesn't mean we're in valentine territory and need to pull out all the stops. It's possible we have nothing in common besides sex."

"That's a damn good start."

"But that's all it is. A start. Let's see how this weekend goes. Right now, I need to give you some space." She kept the beat as she rested her hands on his shoulders and put a couple of inches between them.

"I don't want space." He pressed on the small of her back but she was as unyielding as a department store mannequin.

"The song will be over soon. Then what are you planning to do?"

"Pray for another slow number and a softenin' of your resolve."

"You're a glutton for punishment."

"It's not punishment. More like sweet torture. I'm happy to put up with it."

"I'm not."

"You're hot and bothered, too?"

"Of course I am. What do you suppose happens when I can feel the ridge of your cock?"

His breath caught. "How you talk."

"Just telling it like it is. The longer we stay plastered together on this dance floor, the more I want to take you home with me."

"We could have some fun, Jo." His pulse ramped up at the prospect. "We don't have to advertise what we're doin'. We can leave at different times so it's not obvious that we're meetin' up at your place."

"Sorry, Charlie. Not happening." The song ended and she smiled. "It's been a long, eventful day. I'm going home."

"I'll walk you out."

"No, you won't. If I announce I'm leaving, chances are Mandy and Zane will call it a night. I'll see you on Friday."

"What time?"

"I'll get a ride in to work so you can come to the bank when it closes at five. It's a straight shot from there to the highway."

"Sounds good. Want me to pick up a snack to tide us over?"

"Like what?"

"A couple of hamburgers from the Burger Barn?"

"Great idea."

"I have more where that one came from."

"I'll bet you do." She gave him a quick kiss. "Can't wait to find out what they are."

He stifled a groan of frustration and followed her back to the table. She could find out tonight if she'd loosen up the schedule. Her call, though.

As she'd predicted, when she announced that she was taking off, Mandy and Zane decided to go with her. Ah, well. He'd just order another pint and enjoy watching his brother and Kendra tear up the dance floor. He didn't want a biddable woman. Except sometimes. Like now.

<u>6</u>

Normally Jo wasn't a clock-watcher, but on Friday she glanced at the old-fashioned Regulator on her office wall at least a million times. Midway through the afternoon she stared at the hands to make sure they hadn't stopped.

Two days of agonizing anticipation. No word from Brendan, exactly as she'd requested. A small rolling suitcase sat in a corner of the office, a constant reminder that the hour of reckoning was coming, slowly but surely. What had she been thinking?

On Wednesday night, her plan had made perfect sense. Now, the audacity of it had her pacing the floor and jumping every time the phone buzzed. At ten minutes before five, she ducked into the restroom, checked her makeup and made a face at the wacky woman in the mirror.

She'd done this to herself. Brendan had only asked for a dinner date. She could have accepted his invitation, enjoyed a nice evening on Wednesday and then tootled off for a restful weekend alone. But no.

At five minutes before five, Brendan's cheery greeting to Libby as he entered the lobby sent chills up Jo's spine.

"She's in her office," Libby said. "Just go on back."

"Thanks." His boots thumped rhythmically across the aged hardwood.

Catching a ride to work with Libby and rolling a suitcase into her office had required her to give a quick explanation to her coworkers. Turned out most of them had already known. Not surprising and maybe just as well. As Kendra said on the phone yesterday, *if you're gonna go, go big.*

She returned to her swivel chair and sat down because her legs were a tad wobbly. Her purse lay on her desk and her black coat was draped across the top of her suitcase. She took a deep breath.

"Hey, Jo." A smiling Brendan stood in the doorway, hat in hand.

"Hey, Brendan."

"Ready?"

"Yep." She rolled back her chair and stood. "I just have to get—"

"I see it." He made a move toward her suitcase as she did the same.

"Whoops." He grabbed her shoulders as they collided.

"I can take it." She breathed in the woodsy scent of his aftershave and her stomach did a somersault.

"I know you can." His grip loosened but he didn't release her. "But will you let me?" His voice was soft as a caress.

She gazed into his warm gray eyes. "Let you do what, exactly?"

The corners of his mouth tilted up. "How about everythin'?"

"That's not how I roll."

"I'll narrow it down. Will you let me carry your suitcase to the truck?"

"Yes."

He gave her shoulders a gentle massage. "It's good to see you. These have been the longest two days of—"

"Jo, Mr. Grimes is in the—oh! Excuse me." Libby backed quickly out of the office.

"Don't run off." Jo hurried after her. "What about Mr. Grimes?"

"He came to my window and asked about his loan application." She tucked her blonde hair behind her ears. "Wants to know if we'll have an answer for him by Tuesday."

"Probably, but don't make any promises. Underwriting has been slow recently. Tell him we should have a decision by the end of the week."

"Got it. And my apologies for barging in like that."

"No apology necessary. This is an office. My door was open."

She lowered her voice. "Have a wonderful time, okay?"

"Thanks. I plan to." She smiled. "See you Tuesday morning." When she returned to the office, Brendan was waiting with her coat.

His eyebrows lifted. "Problem?"

"No. Libby can handle it." She slipped her arms into the sleeves and he settled the coat over her shoulders. God, he smelled good. She wanted to turn and bury her nose in the open collar of his Western shirt. Instead she stepped away before facing him while she buttoned her coat. "How cold is it out there?"

"Cold enough to freeze a kangaroo's nu— uh, privates."

She laughed. "Hey, don't censor yourself. I like salty language."

"Good to know. Lot more swearin' goes on Down Under." He put on his hat. "I got in the habit."

"Doesn't bother me." She flipped up her hood, put on her gloves and slung her purse over her shoulder. "We're off." She walked briskly through the lobby so she wouldn't get waylaid by Mr. Grimes, who was still at Libby's window. The elderly widower didn't need a loan as much as he wanted the social interaction involved in applying for one.

Brendan held the door for her and she stepped into the kind of frigid winter evening that sucked the breath from her lungs. Dark gray clouds billowed overhead and the wind tugged at her furry hood.

The new burgundy truck gleamed in the glow of the vintage streetlights lining the sidewalk. "Did you wash it?"

"'Course. Cab should still be warm." He opened the passenger door to reveal a pyramid of Godiva boxes tied with a gold ribbon resting on the leather seat.

"Brendan! You promised not to—"

"Oh, that's not just for you. I plan to gobble up at least half of that choccy. I love me some Godiva." Setting down her suitcase, he whisked the boxes off the seat and offered her a hand up. "Hop in and watch where you put your feet. Burgers are on the floor."

Once she'd buckled up and stowed her purse down by the bag of food, he handed her the candy. "I'll be drivin' so you'll need to take charge of it." He closed the passenger door, leaving her with a lapful of fragrant chocolate and the scent of burgers and fries wafting up from the floor.

He put her suitcase in the back seat. "There's hot coffee in those insulated mugs in the cup holders."

"You've thought of everything."

"Tried to." Closing the back door, he walked around the front of the truck, head bowed and a hand clamped over his hat to keep it on.

Wind and a few snowflakes blew in when he opened the driver's door and climbed in. "Woo-ee! It's workin' up to somethin' out there." He closed the door and swiveled to face her, cheeks ruddy from the cold. "How're you feelin'?"

"Like I'm in the front car of a rollercoaster that's about to blast off."

He grinned. "Me, too. Isn't it great?"

"Yeah." She took a shaky breath. "Yeah, it is."

"Let me relieve you of this." Taking hold of the ribbon, he lifted the boxes from her lap. "I don't expect you to hold it the whole way there."

"Yet you deliberately put it on my seat to begin with."

He deposited it in the back seat as the dome light clicked off, leaving them in the soft gray twilight. "I just relished the drama of havin' you see it first thing."

"Aha! You did get it for me!"

"I got it to impress you, but I'm serious about eating my share."

"I should hope so. That's a ridiculous amount of chocolate."

He glanced at her. "Some folks say it's an aphrodisiac."

That comment found its mark and she shivered in anticipation. "What do you think?"

"Haven't decided yet." His gaze held hers. "Might need to do some testin'. You game?"

Dear Lord, he was potent. "That's....that's what this weekend is all about."

"Which is the understandin' I have." He cleared his throat. "Let's do this thing." Snapping his seat belt into place, he turned the key and the engine roared to life. "Attagirl."

"The truck's female?"

"With this color, yes, ma'am, she sure is." He checked his mirrors and backed out onto Main Street. "I tried out a bold black one that was male through and through, but this sleek beauty stole my heart." He put the truck in gear and pulled away from the bank.

Clenching her gloved hands in her lap, she tamped down a wave of pure lust. Why were they driving two hours through a wintery night? If she asked him to make a different turn, they'd be at her condo in less than ten minutes, naked in five more. No one had to know. They'd think she was out of town... She pressed a hand to her chest and closed her eyes.

"Somethin' wrong?"

"No, no. I'm fine."

"Is the heat turned up too high?"

Yes. "It's fine. I just need to take off my gloves and unbutton my coat."

"Good idea." He drove one-handed while he undid the buttons of his shearling jacket and pulled the lapels aside. "Looked like you were gettin' carsick."

"I don't get carsick."

"Do you need to head home for somethin'? Your road is comin' up."

"How do you know that?"

"Drove over there yesterday, just to see where you lived. Nice complex. Listen, if you forgot somethin', we can swing by there. Wouldn't lose that much time."

"Thanks, but I don't need to go back home."

"Alrighty, then. Off we go." He took the onramp to the divided highway as light snow whirled in the headlights.

Whew. Close call. She didn't want to stay in town for this escapade. A different venue would be much more freeing.

Brendan gestured to the radio. "Volume okay for you?"

"Perfect. Nice background for talking." And now that she was committed to following through with the original plan, a neutral topic of conversation would be good.

She came damned close to asking him about his day. Way too domestic. She could ask why he'd never married. Way too pointed and intense for the beginning of the trip.

The scent of chocolate hung in the air. "When did you order the Godiva?"

"Wednesday night, once I figured out they could get it here by today. Used my phone to go online while I was watchin' Quinn and Kendra out on the floor."

"You didn't ask someone to dance?"

"Thought about it. Any other time, I would've. The band was good."

"What do you mean by *any other time*?"

"I'd accepted your challenge—we either get along this weekend or we call it quits. I used the time to focus on that challenge."

"Interesting."

"Mental preparation makes a huge difference in outcome. I learned that from my Goondeen, which means wise man in the Murri language."

"You spent time with an aboriginal tribe?"

"Some time. Not nearly enough. But that piece of advice was damned clear. When I don't follow it I'm usually sorry, so I stayed in my chair, tapped my foot to the music and concentrated on you."

"Which gave you a chance to order Godiva."

"Yes, ma'am. That's the beauty of their system—expedited delivery."

"Expensive option, though."

"Like I said, it's as much for me as you. Roxanne gave me a box one time when I came back for a visit. Developed a taste for it. Couldn't get it in 'stralia until recently, which made me crave it even more." He chuckled. "For all I know, you don't even like chocolate."

"Your tough luck, I do. Now that I know we'll both be working on that stash, it doesn't look so overwhelming."

"But maybe we should start with the burgers before they get cold."

"Right." She picked up the bag. "Are they both the same?"

"They are. Forgot to ask you what you like on yours, so I ordered the works except for onions. When I'm eatin' with a lady I plan to kiss, I skip those. I've noticed most women do the same."

"Thoughtful of you." She pulled out a warm burger. The wrapping was already moist from the drippings. "Here's a napkin for your lap."

"Thanks." He spread it over his thighs. "Noticed that about these. Even if you keep the wrappin' on, the juice oozes out. But that's what makes 'em good."

"Right. I'll put the fries on the console, but I don't know how you want to work the ketchup."

"I can do without it. Got used to vinegar so now ketchup seems weird. The packets are in there if you want them."

"I'll be lucky if I don't get burger drippings on my clothes. I don't need to wrestle with ketchup packets." Laying a napkin on her lap, she unwrapped the paper halfway and took a bite.

Juice dribbled down her chin, and she grabbed another napkin. "How're you doing over there?"

"Makin' a mess. Need another napkin. Probably should have pulled over to eat this with the snow gettin' thicker."

"How can I help?"

"Hold my burger for a minute."

She plucked it from his outstretched hand. The wrapper had nearly disintegrated. "Maybe we should find a place to pull over."

"I'm lookin' for one. But I haven't seen—shit!" Brendan slammed on the brakes and jerked the wheel as a dark shape bounded in front of the headlights. "Hang on, Jo."

She dropped the burgers in her lap and grabbed the door handle as the truck spun on the icy road. Then it started to slide…

<u>7</u>

Brendan fought the wheel and swore as the truck careened over the slick pavement toward a snow-filled ditch. "No, damn it!" He gave it all he had.

But the momentum generated by the skid sent them hurtling off the road and into the ditch nose first. His butt left the seat as the truck bounced up and rammed into the snowbank on the opposite side with a sickening crunch.

Gasping, he shifted to neutral and took his feet off the pedals. Then he looked over at Jo. "You okay?"

She nodded, eyes wide, face white as the snow outside the window.

"What about your neck? Turn your head for me."

She carefully swiveled it in one direction and then the other.

"Nothing?"

"I'm fine. You?"

"Me, too." He dragged in a breath. "Hope that was ice I heard crunch just now."

"Didn't sound like ice."

"Let's say it was ice."

"What ran in front of us?"

"Large deer or small elk. At least I didn't hit it."

"Think you can get us back on the road?"

"Absolutely. Desiree can handle it."

"Desiree?"

"That's her name." He patted the dash. "Isn't it, girl?"

"I didn't know she had one."

"She didn't until two seconds ago. But Desiree sounds like a woman who can get herself out of a tight spot, and that's what we have here."

"On top of that, our burgers are done for." She gestured toward her lap.

He glanced at the mangled combo of soggy wrappers, squished buns and bits of hamburger and toppings. "They do look a bit nasty. But if we pick out the pieces of wrapping, we could—"

"Use my lap for a serving platter? I don't *think* so, cowboy."

He gave her a slow grin. "Spoilsport."

Her chin came up and a challenge gleamed in her hazel eyes. "Then go for it. I dare you."

He laughed. "Callin' my bluff, are you?"

"Yes, I am."

"You win. I was teasin' you. Now's not the time. I'll help you shovel everything into the bag and be a perfect gentleman in the process."

"Never mind. I'll deal with it. You can search for fries. They went everywhere. You have some on you."

"So I do." Picking them off his thighs and crotch, he dropped them in the bag she'd begun filling with the remains of their burgers. He discovered a few more on the dash and the console.

"I'm about done." She dabbed at her pants with a napkin. "These need to be washed. The resort should have laundry service."

"I can't see any more fries, but I could be sitting on some. I bounced when the truck bounced." He unfastened his seat belt and gripped the wheel. "If I lift up would you check for any squashed ones on the seat or on me?"

"Seriously? You want me to check out your butt?"

"I swear this isn't a sexual maneuver. I don't want to climb out of here with fries stuck to my ass and I don't like the idea of smashin' 'em into the leather."

"I could bring up that speech you made about this being a truck that won't stay perfect, but I won't."

"Thanks. Ready?"

"Yep." She unsnapped her seatbelt and leaned down. "Buns up."

He laughed as he pushed away from the seat. "That's somethin' I don't hear every day."

"Let's hope not. Found one, mashed flat. Oh, and here's a couple more along the back seam. Lift up a little higher, so I can tell whether you have any sticking to your bum."

"I'm runnin' out of headroom."

"Take off your hat."

"Okay." He ducked down and laid it on the dash so he could push up higher. "See anythin'?"

"Quite a bit, actually. Never noticed the super snug fit of your—"

"Hey. *Fries.*"

"Nope, that's it. But I'm enjoying the heck out of this view."

"Show's over. I'm sittin' down."

"Aw, too bad." She straightened and smiled at him.

"You're a handful, lady."

"Don't ever forget it."

"No chance of that. What say we get the hell out of here?"

"I'll vote for that."

"Desiree, I'm counting on you, girl." If he could, he'd move forward some, then back up a little, rocking the vehicle to gain traction. There was no going forward. Might be a rock in that pile of snow.

Nothing to do but engage the four-wheel drive, put the truck in reverse and hope for the best. "Okay, sweetheart, show me what you can do." He checked the side mirror as he pressed gently on the gas. The wheels spun, throwing snow and slush out behind them. The truck didn't budge. "Damn it."

"Now what?"

"Normally I'd carry a shovel and I'd dig out the back wheels so they'd get better traction. But I haven't outfitted this rig yet."

"Bet you have a tire iron." She took off her seat belt and started buttoning her coat.

"Brilliant suggestion, but what do you think you're doing?"

"Going out there with you."

"No, you're not." He put the truck in neutral, got out of his seatbelt and buttoned his coat. "I'll just leave the engine running." He crammed his hat on.

"You don't want to leave the engine running. We might need that gas."

"We're fine on gas. I'll dig us out and we'll be at the resort before you know it. Stay here, please." He opened his door.

"I'm not staying." She opened her door, too.

"Jo, there's nothing for you to do out there!"

She glanced over her shoulder. "I'll offer moral support."

"I don't need—" No point in finishing the sentence. She'd already hopped down and closed the door. "Blasted woman." He turned off the engine and stomped through calf-deep snow to get to the back of the truck.

She was there waiting, her breath fogging the air, her phone in her gloved hand with the flashlight app turned on. "I can also do this so you can see what the hell you're doing."

She had a point about being able to see. It was dark as the inside of a kangaroo's pouch and the snow was falling thick and fast. But he didn't like the idea of her being out in this storm. He was supposed to be treating her like a queen.

She swept the light over the back of the truck. "Where's the tire iron stashed?"

"Behind the back seat on the passenger side." He started in that direction.

She followed, holding her phone high. "I went to the back because I thought it would be stowed there."

"No, ma'am." He opened the door and pulled down the backrest. The salesman had showed him where the jack was or he would have been thumbing through the manual like a dork.

She beamed her flashlight at the opening while he pulled the tire iron out of a case. "Are there more pieces in there? Looks like there are."

"Just extensions. I don't—"

"I could use one to help dig."

He turned to her. "I need you to hold the flashlight."

"I could find a way to prop it up. I—"

"Hey." He cupped his gloved hand behind her head and tugged her closer. Wasn't easy with the slippery material of her hood but he managed. "Let me get us out of this without puttin' you through hard manual labor, okay? The trip is supposed to be a relaxin' getaway, not some episode of *Survivor*."

Her warm breath touched his face. "I want to help."

"I know, but lettin' you shovel snow with a piece of a tire iron would hurt my soul."

"That's testosterone talking."

"And so is this." He kissed her cold lips. None of her should be cold, yet here they were, standing in a damned snowstorm. Not the way he wanted this to go.

Her mouth warmed and softened beneath his. Good to know she still wanted him, even if he had dumped them in a ditch. Too bad he couldn't keep kissing her but they had stuff to do. He lifted his head and sighed. "We'll get back to that. I promise."

"I believe you."

"Aim the flashlight toward the right tire. I'll start there."

She lowered the beam to the snow behind the tire. "How's that?"

"Perfect." He scraped and chipped until his arms ached. Maybe that was enough. "Now the other side." He repeated the process, digging at the frozen ground as best he could factoring in the limitations of the tool in his hand. "Let's try it."

"This will work."

"Sure hope so." He walked her to the passenger side, helped her in and handed her the keys. "Start the engine to get the heat going." Then he slid the tire iron onto the floor of the backseat and headed around to the driver's side.

This *had* to work. Surely he wouldn't be given a golden opportunity to spend quality time with Jo only to have it snatched away by a freak accident. Maybe this was a test. His Goondeen would likely say it was.

If so, he was determined to pass it with flying colors. Before long they'd be stretched out on a luxury mattress sipping champagne and working up to the big moment when they'd actually be able to...better not think about it.

Sliding behind the wheel, he closed the door and put on his seatbelt. "Thank you for goin' out there with me."

"I couldn't let you go by yourself. Even if you hadn't needed the flashlight, it wouldn't have been right to sit here with the heater blasting while you were out there freezing your fanny and trying to get us loose."

"I would have been fine with that."

"Really?"

"Yea, yea. Definitely." He put the truck in reverse.

"I'm not some delicate flower you have to protect from the big bad world."

"I know. It's one of the things I admire about you. And yet...when push comes to shove, I hate the idea of you standin' out in the bitter cold while you help me with this issue."

"So you admire my self-sufficiency but you'd rather I didn't ever have to use it?"

"Somethin' like that."

"Oh, boy."

"What's that supposed to mean?"

"It means we have to talk, but not now."

"Right. Not now." He took a deep breath and focused on the rear tires as he pressed slowly on the gas. Another damn rooster tail.

He clamped his back teeth together and held back all the words he'd learned to employ in situations like this. Salty language was one thing. But after all those years Down Under, he could pickle a person's eardrums.

"What now?"

"We need a tow."

"We'll call Quinn."

"No."

"No? He's the logical—"

"I'm not askin' my brother to drive out here tonight in an effin' snowstorm to pull my ass out of a ditch."

She gazed at him in silence for a moment. "Do you have roadside assistance?"

"No, ma'am. I decided against that option when I bought this. Maybe I should've—"

"Hey, I get why you didn't. You know a gazillion helpful people with trucks. I even get why you're reluctant to call Quinn. I'll call Zane. He loves helping people. He'd be more than happy to—"

"I don't want to call him, either."

"Then you suggest somebody. You have three strong, healthy nephews in town. I'm sure one of them would come out here."

"I'm sure they would, but—"

A horn beeped and headlights focused on the back of the truck. A male voice yelled something.

Brendan put down his window and leaned out. "What's that?"

"Looks like you need a tow!"

"Sure do, mate!"

"We can do that!"

"Excellent!" He turned to Jo. "See? We'll be on our way in no time. And I didn't have to call anybody out here."

"They would have been glad to come."

"Maybe so, but this is better."

She gave him a look that said she doubted it.

"It is. You'll see. This is going to work out fine. Before you know it, we'll be at the resort enjoyin' a nice dinner."

8

Jo stayed in the truck while Brendan got out to talk with their would-be rescuer. Probably it would all be fine, just like he'd said, and she hadn't relished the idea of dragging a loved one away from a cozy evening, either. But she would have done it because that's how folks operated in Eagles Nest. They helped one another, and were miffed if you didn't ask. Insulted, even.

The storm was getting worse by the minute, though, and having someone come along and pull them out now was a faster option. Loud male voices and hearty laughter were punctuated by clanking and scraping noises.

Then Brendan opened the door and got behind the wheel. "Couple of really nice guys." He shut the door and put the truck in neutral. "Live not too far from here. On their way home when they spotted us."

"That's lucky."

"Sure is." Snow clung to his hat and the shoulders of his coat. "I have to put down the window so we can communicate."

"Understood." She was still bundled up, anyway.

"Better buckle up, too."

"Okay."

He stuck his head out the window. "All set, mate! Take 'er away!"

The other truck's engine growled as the chain rattled and pulled taut. Brendan's truck jerked and eased slowly backward.

"Easy, Desiree. Easy, girl."

With loud crackling and crunching, the truck's grill parted ways with the snowbank.

"Keep goin'!" Brendan called out the window. "A little more, a little more...okay, stop!" He studied the light reflecting off the snowbank. "Lost the right headlight."

"I see that."

"And we hit a rock."

"I see that, too." Parts of a jagged gray boulder protruded from the mounded snow. "If you want to swear, go ahead."

"No point in swearin' yet. Might not be that bad. Let me take a looksee."

Instead of announcing her intention to go with him like last time, she just got out, phone in hand, flashlight activated. He arrived first and groaned in dismay.

She plowed through drifts and trained her light on the front of the truck. "Oh, Brendan."

"Yea, yea, not good." He stared at the truck, gloved hands shoved in his pockets without saying anything more.

She would have preferred a fiery string of curses. He hadn't had the truck long, but as he'd said, he'd fallen in love. And now Desiree's front grill was caved in as if she'd been punched in the mouth. Poor girl.

"How's it look?" A burly man in a red parka stepped into the light from the left headlamp. "Ouch. That's gonna blow right past the deductible. Sorry, buddy."

"What's the sitch?" A second guy, built much like the first but wearing a brown parka, joined the group. "Yikes."

Brendan gestured toward the snowbank. "Rock."

"Yeah, they're all along this stretch." The man in red waved an arm toward the highway. "Had to blast through some places to make the road and stuff's still shaking loose."

Brendan heaved a sigh. "So I see." He reached out a hand to Jo and drew her closer. "Jo Fielding, I'd like you to meet Andy Culbertson , the guy in the red, and his brother Seth, the one in the brown."

"Pleased to meet you both." She stepped toward them and each man took off his glove before shaking hands with her. Sweet. "Thanks for stopping."

"Glad to do it." Andy put on his glove. "A shame about your trip, though. Brendan said you were headed toward that new resort over in Anaconda."

"That's right."

"Won't get there tonight, I'm afraid."

"Is the truck that bad?"

"It's not so much the damage to the truck, but there's a wreck—"

"If you ask me," Seth cut in, "this truck is not roadworthy, never mind the wreck up ahead. A knocked-out headlight's a problem, but I'll bet there's considerable radiator damage, too."

Brendan winced. "Hope you're wrong."

"I hope so, too, but you don't want to take chances on a night like this."

"Not to mention the wreck." Andy pulled out a cell phone, tapped it and swore under his breath. "Phone gets an attitude when it's cold and wet, but take my word for it. Bad pileup between here and there."

"Yeah," Seth said. "Happened about fifteen minutes ago, right before we saw you guys. We have a scanner. Picks up all the cop talk. All lanes shut down."

Jo glanced at Brendan. "Maybe we could head back to Eagles Nest, pick up my car and by then the road might be open."

"I really hate to see you get back on the road without checking to see if the radiator's compromised." Seth gazed at the smashed front grill. "I don't see how it couldn't be."

"I agree," Brendan said, "but that doesn't leave us any options."

"We might have one." Andy looked over at his brother. "That cabin's probably in decent shape."

"Might be, at that. It's no resort, but they'd have a bed. Not sure about the fireplace, but—"

"That's okay." Whatever they were offering sounded dicey as hell to Jo. "We'll nurse the truck back to Eagles Nest."

Andy shook his head. "Wouldn't advise it. Seth knows his trucks and he's seen his share of wrecked ones. We call him the truck whisperer. If he says your radiator's in trouble, that means it's ready to go to radiator heaven. I doubt you want to follow it there."

Jo faced Brendan with a steady gaze, telegraphing her wishes as best she could. "Then we leave the truck here, call Quinn or Zane or somebody in the family to come get us. We'll have the truck towed and set out for the resort in my SUV in the morning."

"Up to you," Andy said, "but with it snowing this hard, it could take them a long time to get here from Eagles Nest. The roads are slick as glass as you just found out. Personally, I wouldn't want to ask a friend or relative to—"

"You're right and we won't ask." Brendan wiped melted snow off his face with his coat sleeve. "Not while the storm's blowin' like this."

She nodded. Maybe the cabin they'd mentioned wouldn't be too awful and it was only for one night.

Brendan turned toward the brothers. "We'll take your generous offer and get help in the mornin'."

"Might not need to." Seth shoved his hands in his pockets and rocked back on his heels, seemingly oblivious to the weather. "You could have a working vehicle by noon if that radiator's not totally DOA. Got myself a little repair shop on the property. I'd consider it a personal challenge to get you two lovebirds back on the road tomorrow."

Jo blinked. "Lovebirds?"

"Gotta be. You have reservations at a swanky resort the weekend after Valentine's Day." He tilted his head toward Brendan. "Your sweetheart bought a new truck for the journey. Nothing says romance like purchasing a new truck."

Jo was at a loss. How to respond when Seth was partially right?

Brendan put an arm around her shoulders. "I'm very fond of this woman, mate, and I'd like to get her out of this weather ASAP."

"We all need to get out of this weather," Andy said. "We'll tow you to our place. Not far. You can squeeze in with us."

"*Oh.*" She hadn't thought that far.

Seth glanced at her. "Not safe to be in that truck while we're towing it, ma'am. Too much margin for error. We got us a crew cab. It's—"

"You can ride up front with me, ma'am," Andy said. "We can squash Seth and Brendan in the back."

"I'm the smallest person so it's not right for me to take the front seat. I'll ride in back with Brendan."

Seth chuckled. "Could be cozy, at that."

"I just need to grab my purse out of the truck."

"I'll get it." Brendan gave her shoulder a squeeze before heading toward the passenger side.

"Real shame about his truck," Andy said. "It'll need some body work. Unfortunately we're not set up for that, which you'll know the minute you catch sight of our old girl."

"Decent body shop can make this beauty good as new." Seth adjusted the hood of his parka. "Still, it's tough to see something so pretty get banged up."

"It is tough, mate." Brendan came back and handed Jo her purse. "But nobody was hurt. That's the important thing."

"That's the best way to look at it." Andy tugged the zipper of his parka up to his chin and turned into the wind. "You'll want to climb in on Seth's side. Got a chicken on my side. She's in a cage, though. Just put her on your lap and she'll be fine."

"I'll take the chicken." Brendan grinned at Jo as they approached Andy and Seth's battered truck. A tarp was laced down over what looked like hay bales. "Unless you want to."

"I'll be glad to hold her. I like chickens." She took satisfaction from his surprised expression.

"My mom's crazy about 'em." Seth opened the passenger door and flipped the seat back so they could climb in.

Brendan hesitated. "Did you really want to hold the chicken?"

"Sure, why not?"

"Then in you go."

She squeezed into the cramped back seat, picked up the covered cage and sat down on the threadbare upholstery. Fluttering noises came from under the towel draped over the cage as she settled it on her lap. "Does she have a name?"

"We'll let Mom name her." Andy got behind the wheel and slammed the door, which caused more fluttering. "We picked her up from an ol' boy who lives outside of Bozeman. Mom's gonna love her. She lays colored eggs."

"She's an Easter Egger, then?"

"Yes, ma'am. You know chickens?"

"Not as well as my best friend Kendra does."

"So that's how you came to like chickens." Brendan shoehorned himself into the seat. His knees nearly touched his chest. "I was wonderin'. What's an Easter Egger look like?"

"They're all different," Andy said. "This one's feathers are a pretty shade of orange. Mom likes orange."

"She *loves* orange." Seth slammed his door, too, creating more nervous fluttering in the cage. "Hang on. Didn't catch." He opened it and slammed it again. This time the chicken gave a squawk of annoyance. "Sorry, chickie."

"Keep an eye on our tow, Seth."

"Yep." Seth focused on his side-view mirror. "Following along like a baby duck. A big, burgundy baby duck. Say that six times, Andy."

Andy sighed. "Not saying it, Seth."

"Because you can't, that's why." Seth proceeded to rattle it off six times. "Nailed it."

Jo cleared her throat to keep from giggling. "You keep mentioning your mom. I take it she lives on your place, too?"

"Technically we live on her place." Seth maintained his surveillance of Brendan's truck. "Still doing good, Andy."

"Keep watching. And speaking of Mom, we need to settle something before we get there. You two don't have the same last name. Does that mean you're not married?"

"That's right," Brendan said. "We're not."

"Is it okay if I introduce you as Jo and Brendan Sawyer, anyway?"

"How come?"

"Mom's a bit old-fashioned. Back when we were renting out that cabin to travelers, she wouldn't rent to a couple unless they were married. Since we're bringing you home to spend the night, she'll expect that we've checked that out. If you'd be willing to pretend that you are, that would help."

Jo looked at Brendan. "Think we can pull that off?"

"Guess so. I'll take my cues from you. I don't have any practice in behavin' like a married man."

"Are you kidding me?" Seth glanced over his shoulder. "That can't be right."

"It's true, mate."

"Engaged?"

"Nope."

"Hard to believe, at your age."

Brendan coughed. "Yea, yea, but I just never—"

"I mean, you seem like a nice enough guy and you're not bad to look at. You're fit, too, more so than Andy and me. How is it that you never got married?"

Great question. Jo had wanted to ask but hadn't worked up to it yet. Thanks to Seth, the subject was on the table.

And Brendan was squirming. "Well, the thing is, I—"

"C'mon, Seth." Andy blew out a breath. "You're getting too personal. What if he has issues he'd rather not discuss with you?"

"Like what?"

"You know. *Issues.*"

"What kind of...oh. I get it. Sorry, dude."

Jo gulped back laughter as she peeked over at Brendan.

He winked at her. "No worries, mate."

Sexy wink. Sexy guy. Great kisser. Why hadn't he ever married? She needed the answer. And she'd get it before the weekend was over.

9

Andy had saved Brendan from repeating the same bullshit he dished out to everybody. His mates over in Australia had quit asking, but he was in a new place and the question would start coming at him again. He was surprised Jo hadn't asked it.

I just never found the right woman. How arrogant was that? He winced every time he said it but he didn't have a better way of shutting down that line of questioning. Hell, he'd found a bunch of great women. He'd never been the right man. Still might not be. Time would tell.

Looked like he'd have a chance to play-act at being married for a little while, though. Should be an interesting exercise.

The road to Andy and Seth's place was considerably rougher than the highway. He turned so he could look out the back window.

"It'll be okay."

He glanced at Jo. "Bouncin' around like a whacked-out wallaby. If that chain gives way…"

"It won't."

He couldn't see her expression very well but she sounded completely certain. "How do you know?"

She lowered her voice, although the noise from the trucks and the rattling chain likely made it unnecessary. "We're in good hands."

He smiled. "Yea, yea, I like them, too. All right. I'll relax."

"Are you hungry?"

"I could eat. You?"

"Yes. I guess there's always Godiva, but—"

"You don't want to fill up on that. I gorged myself on them once. Sicker'n a dog for hours."

"I'll bet. I wonder if we could ask for a sandwich when we get there."

"I think that'd be all right. I'd already planned to give them some money for the trouble and expense of this."

"Assuming they'll take it. I'm not sure they will. At the very least, we could give them some of the Godiva."

"Good idea. Which one?"

"The big one on the bottom? Maybe the next biggest one, too."

He nodded. "Sounds good. They saved our bacon out there." The truck hit a particularly large bump and the chicken squawked.

Jo leaned over the cage. "It's okay, sweetie. You're fine. You're going to a good home."

"I hear you guys murmuring back there," Andy said. "I'm taking a wild guess that you didn't get dinner."

"Not much of one," Brendan said. "So maybe if we could have somethin' easy, like a sandwich, that would—"

"Forget sandwiches." Seth turned around. "I already texted Mom and said we were bringing home a nice married couple who ran into a snowbank and got stranded. Told her the husband sounds like Crocodile Dundee."

"No, I don't."

Jo laughed. "Yes, you do."

"She's right, you do." Seth turned around and checked the side-view mirror. "Anyway, Mom's warming up a big pot of beef stew."

"Sounds fabulous," Jo said.

"You don't know the half of it. She's a great cook. That's why Andy and me look the way we do. She'll have homemade bread to go with the stew and apple pie for dessert. With ice cream. When we were renting out the cabin, the guests raved about the food."

Brendan's stomach rumbled. "Why did you stop rentin' it out?"

"We were losing money," Andy said. "Mom was spending a fortune on feeding our guests but she wouldn't let us charge enough for the cabin to cover it. Not sure we could have gotten top dollar, anyway. The cabin's not plush and we're off the beaten path."

"You won't be losin' money on us. I'll happily pay whatever you need so you're not out anythin'."

Andy shook his head. "Nope, you're not allowed to pay for the cabin or the meals. If Seth fixes your truck so it's drivable, you can pay him something. We're not taking money for food and lodging after we invited you to stay with us."

"But—"

"Seriously, dude." Seth turned to look at him. "What Andy said. Don't try to pay. You'll just get us upset."

Under cover of darkness, Jo reached over and squeezed his thigh. He sucked in a breath and covered her hand with his. "Don't mean to insult you, mate." Likely she was only signaling him to leave the payment issue alone. But one touch from her and fire licked through his veins.

She was holding a chicken on her lap, for God's sake, and still he wanted to haul her into his arms and kiss her until she couldn't see straight. That would cause a major problem in this tiny backseat for both them and the chicken, so he settled for lifting her hand to his lips and nibbling on her fingers.

Her breathing changed. Even with the growl of the truck's motor and the racket his truck was making as it bounced along the bumpy road, he could tell she was affected.

By now they should have been tucked into a luxury room at the resort. He'd be kissing way more than her fingers. She'd be breathing even faster as he...damn it. No point in fantasizing the alternative to what they had—an offer of shelter and two generous young guys eager to help. He was grateful, incredibly so, but—

"We're here." Andy announced their arrival with pride as he parked in front of a two-story farmhouse with lights glowing through lace-curtained windows. "After we eat, Seth and I will help you carry your luggage over to the cabin."

"We'll do it." Brendan glanced at Jo, who gave him a quick nod. "We only have overnight bags."

"You can carry them if you want." Seth opened his door, the dome light came on and the chicken fluttered in her cage. "But we'll need to come with you and check the condition of the cabin." He climbed down and lowered the seatback. "Just pass me that chicken and then you two can come on out."

Jo adjusted the towel over the cage. "I don't think she likes the cold air."

"Don't worry." Andy opened his door and hopped down. "She'll be in a heated henhouse tonight. I just want to show her to Mom first. Seth, you want to take her in?"

"Nah, you can. It was your idea to buy her on this trip."

Brendan got out and helped Jo down. "Before I go inside, I want to get somethin' out of the truck."

Seth handed the chicken cage to his brother. "In that case, might as well get your luggage, too. I'll go with you."

"Good idea," Andy said. "Jo, want to come inside with me?"

"I'll stay with Brendan. I want to check with him about something."

"Then I'll hustle this chicken inside." He started for the front porch.

Brendan took Jo's hand as they started back toward the truck. Seth fell into step on her other side. Now that Seth was here, might as well find out if the Godiva would be a hit. "Does your mom like chocolate?"

"Oh, man, does she ever. Especially those sampler boxes with the diagram on the inside of the lid so you know exactly what you're getting."

"Would a chart with a picture of each one work, too?"

"Probably would. She just likes identifying what she's biting into."

"Then Jo and I would like to give her some chocolate we brought with us."

"That's a really nice idea. Thanks for thinking of her."

"You bet." He'd left the truck unlocked, but when he grabbed the handle of the back door, it wouldn't budge.

"Guess it froze," Seth said.

"Guess so." He put his back into it. The door popped open with a sound like the crack of a rifle and the dome light flicked on, illuminating the stack of Godiva boxes.

"Holy hell!" Seth's eyes widened. "You're giving her all that?"

Sending a silent apology to Jo, Brendan picked up the whole shebang. "Yes, we are." He gave the tower of candy to Seth. "It's the least we can do."

"These look fancy." He glanced at Jo. "Were they for you?"

She shook her head. "Not exactly. Brendan bought them for both of us, and we've agreed we want to give them to your mother. I imagine she'll share with both of you."

"Oh, she will." His round face glowed. "Good candy like this, she'll ration us to one piece a day, which is fine." He unzipped his parka. "Better tuck it inside or the ribbon will—"

"Head on up to the house with it," Brendan said. "We'll be right behind you."

"Okay. I'll wait for you on the porch." Sheltering the chocolate as best he could, he hurried off.

"That was brilliant." Jo's eyes sparkled. "I'm so glad you gave him the whole thing."

"Had to. Cheated you out of some truffles, though."

"I don't care. Did you see the look on his face?"

"Yea, yea, I did." He was enjoying the look on her face even more. Wouldn't mind kissing her, but it was damned cold and Seth was waiting on the porch. Turning back to the truck, he grabbed his large duffle in one hand, leaned across the seat and picked up Jo's overnighter in the other.

"I'll take that." She reached for it.

He smiled and pulled it out of reach. "No, you won't. We established that I could carry your suitcase. But I'd be obliged if you'd shut the door."

She pushed it shut. "Done."

"Then let's—"

"Hang on. We need to talk about my ring."

"What ring?"

"If we're supposed to be married, I should probably be wearing one. I don't even have one on a different finger that I could switch over to my left hand."

"Ah, I get it. I have one on my pinky finger that might work."

"I don't remember you wearing one."

"I wasn't on Wednesday. I put it on for this trip."

"Why?"

"It's supposed to help me see things more clearly."

"What?"

"Tribal thing. My Goondeen gave it to me before I left 'stralia."

"That's very cool, Brendan. And special. I wouldn't feel right wearing it."

"It won't hurt for you to pretend it's your wedding ring until we get out of here tomorrow. Assumin' it fits." He set down their luggage and pulled off the glove on his right hand. "We're only talkin' a few hours."

"Hm." She gazed at him. "But it's your talisman. I just—"

"Try it on." He wiggled the ring loose. "If it fits, we won't have to make up a story about why you're not wearin' one."

"True. I guess I could at least see if it fits." She took off her glove. "Of course you won't have a wedding band on your left hand, either."

"I can say I don't wear one because it's dangerous in my line of work."

"Is it?"

He shrugged. "Who knows? I've heard stories that they catch on stuff but I've never tested that. Never had a ring until my Goondeen gave me this one." He handed it to her.

"Looks like pewter."

"It is."

"I like that. It's different." She slid it on her third finger. "Huh. Perfect fit." She peered at the ring. "What's that etched into it?"

"A crocodile. My spirit animal."

"See? You're not so far off from Crocodile Dun—"

"I'm nothin' like him."

"So you say." She glanced into his eyes and her smile faded. "Brendan, I'm honored that you've trusted me with this."

"No worries. We need to get goin'. Seth's waitin'."

She took a deep breath and pulled on her glove. "I'll take really good care of it."

"I know you will or I wouldn't have given it to you."

"Loaned it to me."

"Right."

<u>10</u>

Jo hadn't worn a ring since she'd taken off her diamond engagement ring and wedding band when she and Robert divorced more than twelve years ago. She wasn't much of a jewelry person so what was the point? The familiar sensation of a metal band circling the base of her finger, especially that significant one, was unsettling.

Seth stood by the glass storm door waiting. "Everything okay?"

"I figured out I needed a wedding ring."

He nodded. "Yeah, and I didn't think of that, so I'm glad you did. She notices those little details."

Not a comforting bit of info. Jo couldn't speak for Brendan, but lying didn't come naturally to her and their story was flimsy.

"What'd you and Brendan do about it?"

"I loaned her the one I was wearin' on my pinky."

"Whew. Nice save, dude." Seth handed him the Godiva. "Didn't get too wet, just a couple of spots. I'll go first and let her know you're coming in." After thoroughly wiping his boots on the mat, he opened the storm door and then the sturdy wooden one. "The guests are here, Mom!"

Jo stepped onto the mat and scrubbed the soles of her boots on the nubby material as best she could. Then she glanced at Brendan. "Ready?"

He took off his hat and swept it toward the open door. "After you, my love."

The endearment knocked the breath out of her. She gave him a startled glance.

He smiled and lifted his eyebrows as if to say *somethin' wrong?*

Oh, right. Some husbands talked to their wives that way. Not Robert, though, and he was the only guy she'd seriously dated. No man had ever called her his love until now. Brendan was only play-acting, but he was too damn good at it. Freaked her out.

She walked into a house filled with mouth-watering aromas—beef stew, freshly baked bread and coffee. Underlying that was the tangy scent of lemon oil. Antique furniture in the living room gleamed as if their hostess had run around with polish and a dust rag while the stew was heating.

Mrs. Culbertson emerged from the kitchen wiping her hands on a frilly apron. She was tiny, less than five feet, and her bouffant hairstyle, flared skirt and bright orange blouse were straight out of the fifties.

Andy and Seth's comments had made her sound elderly, but the woman who hurried to greet them was around Jo's age. She didn't dress like it, though. Instead she appeared to be caught in a time warp.

Smiling as if they were old friends, she held out her hand. "I'm Ida Culbertson. It's Jo, right?"

"Jo Fielding...Sawyer." Geez. Screwing up already. She resisted the urge to crouch a little as she shook Ida's small hand. "And this is my h-husband, B-Brendan." She sucked at this.

Ida's brown eyes widened as she looked at Brendan. "Lord have mercy! What do you have there?"

"My wife and I would like to give you this chocolate as a thank-you for taking us in."

*My wife and I...*that echo from the past sent a shiver up her spine. The words didn't reflect reality and they were spoken with an Australian accent, but they still shook her and not in a good way.

"My goodness, you *do* sound like Crocodile Dundee. And that's not mere *chocolate*! That's *Godiva.*"

"Yes, ma'am. And we—"

"You didn't just happen to have that with you, Mr. Sawyer from Australia. You obviously gave it to your lovely wife for Valentine's Day and she decided to bring it along for your Valentine's weekend." She crossed her arms. "It's very generous, but I really can't accept it."

"Oh, please do." Jo unbuttoned her coat. "Andy said you won't take payment for putting us up, and—"

"Certainly not! He invited you here."

"Which is lovely, but we won't feel right about accepting your hospitality unless we can give you something special, too. We want you to have the chocolate. Please take it with our blessing."

"Well, I don't know..."

"You'll make us feel better about imposing on you."

"It's not an imposition." Her expression grew wistful. "I loved it when we had guests, although I never did get that cabin decorated the way I wanted to."

"Please take the chocolate."

"All right, if it'll make you feel good about staying. That's my goal for anyone who comes through my door."

Maybe all Ida needed was a revised business strategy. Clearly she enjoyed taking in guests. Seemed a shame she wasn't doing it anymore.

Brendan held up the stack of boxes. "Where would you like me to put these, Mrs. Culbertson?"

"You can call me Ida, and I'll take them into the kitchen. Seth, hang their coats in the closet and show them where they can wash up. Dinner will be ready in five minutes."

"Yes, ma'am." Seth waited until she'd gone back to the kitchen. "Thanks for sticking to your guns. That candy will be a big treat and she doesn't get a whole lot of those."

Jo had a million questions. Helping people make good business decisions was her job and she was itching to figure out a solution for this woman who was a born innkeeper. Her two supportive sons would work to make it a success if they knew what to do.

Seth led them down to a bathroom in the hall that was dated but spotless and left them to wash up for dinner.

Brendan leaned in the doorway to the bathroom while she washed her hands in the sink. "Are you okay?"

"I'm fine." She glanced over at him. "Why?"

"You were lookin' agitated earlier, like a dingo who'd shoved his nose in an anthill."

She lowered her voice. "It's the marriage thing. Hearing you refer to me as your wife is—"

"Weird. I know. I couldn't believe it was comin' out of my mouth. I've never thought in terms of havin' a wife."

"You don't have one."

"I do until we drive away from here."

"No, you don't." She dried her hands on a towel hanging near the sink. "It's only make-believe." She stepped back. "All yours."

He traded places with her, rolled up his sleeves and turned on the water. "If I'm goin' to sound authentic, I need to tell myself it's real. Otherwise I'll mess up."

She stared at him. "You're telling yourself it's real?"

"Have to." He lathered up. "Ida Culbertson is a very nice lady. She's bought the story and I don't want her to ever find out we lied to her. So I'm immersin' myself in the truth as she knows it." He rinsed his hands, turned off the water and glanced at her. "We're married."

She swallowed. "No, we're not."

"I don't know why you're so scared of the idea." He dried his hands on the towel. "You've been married before. I should be the one having the heebie jeebies. I've never taken that walk down the aisle."

"Why not?"

His movements slowed and he carefully replaced the towel. Then he met her gaze. "If we're goin' to spend time together, you deserve a decent answer to that. And I don't have one. Not yet."

"Fair enough."

"Why does pretendin' to be married have you so riled up?"

"Because married life wasn't much fun and it ended in total humiliation. I don't relish going through that again."

"Would you be willin' to tell me about it sometime?"

"Sometime. Maybe. I don't consider it a good topic for this weekend, though. Major buzz kill."

He grinned. "Which would be a cryin' shame since the weekend's been perfect so far."

That made her laugh.

"Don't know about you, but my buzz is still goin' strong."

Smiling, she moved into the bathroom and slid her palms up his chest. "Mine, too."

"Excellent." He pulled her close. "Tell you what. Once we're naked and exhausted from makin' love, you can tell me all about the jerk you married."

"What if I don't want to?"

Leaning down, he brushed his mouth over hers. "I'll coax it out of you with some more good lovin'. Like my Goondeen says, bottlin' up stuff only makes it grow stronger."

"This Goondeen fellow of yours is—"

"Dinner's on the table, folks!" Seth's voice echoed in the hallway. "Get it while it's hot!"

"Don't I wish I could." He kissed her hard and released her. "Fuel up, lady. You'll be needin' it tonight."

11

After Ida said grace, Brendan tucked into one of the best beef stews he'd ever tasted. He slathered homemade bread with plenty of Ida's special honey butter and accepted her offer of a second helping of stew.

Ida beamed at him from her place at the head of the antique table. Her orange blouse matched the flowers in the tablecloth. In fact, her blouse matched most things in the house—drapes, throw pillows, pictures on the wall.

"Great meal, Ida."

"Thank you. Does my heart good to see a man enjoy his food the way you do." She glanced past him to Jo. "You must love cooking for him."

"I've never—"

"She's a great cook." Brendan nudged her knee under the table. "But I'm not so bad in the kitchen, myself. Cookin' together can be fun."

Ida nodded. "Both my boys can cook up a storm, too. You should see the three of us in the kitchen during canning season. Poetry in motion."

"I love canning season." Andy scooped the last of his stew from the bowl. "Putting up all those fruits and veggies is satisfying. The money's nice, but I'd want to do it even if we didn't earn anything on the deal."

Jo put down her coffee mug. "You sell your canned goods?"

"Yes, ma'am." Andy nodded. "We set up a stand out on the main road, which works great when the weather's decent. Can't very well do it this time of year, though."

"I'll bet it's tasty," Brendan said. "I wouldn't mind buyin' a few things while we're here, if you have any left."

"Me, too," Jo said. "I like keeping my pantry stocked with special things like—"

"I know you do, honey." He bumped her knee again. "That's why I suggested buyin' some. I knew you'd be salivatin' over the idea of homemade canned goods lined up in that big ol' pantry of ours."

She turned to him, clearly trying not to laugh. "You know me so well, sweetheart."

"Always more to learn, though." He gave her a wink that brought color to her cheeks.

"We'll give you whatever you want," Ida said. "We have more than we can eat this winter and we won't be selling this year's crop next summer. That wouldn't be right."

Jo glanced at her. "You end up with an excess?"

"Usually."

"Always," Andy said. "Montana doesn't have a very long growing season, but luckily Mom and I were blessed with a green thumb."

"Not me." Seth picked up another piece of bread and spread it with honey butter.

"But you're a whiz at anything mechanical," Ida said. "Which will come in handy when it comes to fixing Brendan and Jo's truck."

Brendan and *Jo's* truck? He did a mental double-take. Ah. Married people shared ownership of things—vehicles, houses, furniture. When he and Quinn had been cash-strapped teens, they'd jointly owned a truck. That hadn't gone well.

Maybe when you were married to someone that kind of thing worked out better. He'd been eager to let Jo drive his new truck. Then again, he'd wanted to impress her so she'd go out with him. It wasn't like he'd offered to put her on the title.

Seth finished off his slice of bread. "I hope I can fix it."

"I hope so, too." Ida gazed at Brendan. "How sad that you and Jo had that wreck on your special weekend."

"But at least Andy and Seth came along. Without them we would have been sunk. Hardly anyone on the highway. Their timin' was perfect."

"You can thank Reba for that," Ida said.

He stared at her in confusion. "Who's Reba?"

"My chicken. Once I saw what color she is, I named her Reba. I love her music. And her hair. Wish I looked good as a redhead, but I don't. Barring that, I wish I looked good with my hair natural, like yours, Jo. And short, too. Must make life a lot easier."

"It does. I can be ready for work in no time at all."

"Where do you work?"

"I'm a loan officer at the Eagles Nest Bank."

"You must be great with numbers and spreadsheets, then. I'm terrible when it comes to that, and the boys aren't much better."

"That's when you come and talk to someone like me."

Brendan gave her another nudge under the table. The direction of the conversation could get her in trouble really fast.

"I probably should," Ida said.

Oh, boy. Here we go.

"Do you have a card, Jo?"

"I do. It's in my—"

"No, it's not, honey. Remember our deal? You left your cards at home. This trip is supposed to be all pleasure and no business."

Jo slapped her forehead. "You are so right. I promised I wouldn't talk business with anyone and now I'm doing it. Sorry, dearest."

"No worries." Brendan put his arm around her shoulders and gave her a kiss on the cheek. "I know how you love your job."

"That's so sweet." Ida gave them an approving smile. "Both of you leaving work behind to concentrate on each other."

"That's the plan." And the sooner they were alone, the better, for many reasons. He turned to Andy. "Weren't you goin' to tell us about the cabin?"

"Right. I wanted to brief you before we head down there."

"It's rough around the edges," Ida said. "I had plans to make it real cute, but we didn't have the funds. If we had room here, I'd—"

"The cabin will be fine." He'd be alone with Jo, which would make it way more than fine.

"It can be cozy if you build a fire, but…" Her voice trailed off.

"I'll fill them in, Mom." Andy gave her a smile.

"All right." Ida pushed back her chair. "Seth and I will dish the pie. Does everyone want ice cream on it?"

He was full, but not too full for pie a la mode. "I'd be much obliged."

"Me, too." Jo got up. "I'll help Ida and Seth while you get the deets."

Once they'd left, Andy leaned back in his chair. "Just a few things to be aware of. The hot water heater tank is a little on the small side, so shower quick."

"Got it." So much for fooling around in the shower.

"Like Mom said, it's not fancy. We'll have to take a vacuum down there, too. It's not airtight and dust blows in. Bound to be some cobwebs. Will any of that bother Jo? Is she a neat freak?"

"Probably not."

"What's her place like?"

"Never been in it."

"How long have you been dating?"

"We've never dated. We're just gettin' started."

Andy's eyes widened and he lowered his voice "You haven't done the deed?"

"Not yet."

"Good grief. No wonder you've slipped up a few times. You barely know each other."

"It's not like it sounds. We're more connected than that. It's not like I met her yesterday."

"When?"

"At Christmas."

"Okay. That's a couple of months."

"Not really. I was in 'stralia for most of that time. I flew back last weekend."

"Like I said, you barely know each other. Bold move, dude, heading off for a weekend with a woman before you've even—"

"Her idea."

"Get out of here."

"Seriously. She suggested it."

"Guess you're more of a stud than I thought. How'd you meet her?"

"Her best friend Kendra, the one who has chickens, is my brother's..." He paused. How to describe that relationship? "Kendra and my brother Quinn are as good as married, but they haven't...I mean, they love each other very much and are absolutely committed, but—"

"Look, don't try to explain any of that to my mother. Ever. In her world, you're either married in the eyes of God or you're not."

"I respect that. For the record, I don't like pretendin' we're somethin' we're not."

"I know, but if she learned the truth, you'd be spending the night alone in the cabin and Jo would be sharing Mom's bed. I doubt you want that."

"Uh, no. No, I don't."

"Don't worry. If the story comes apart, I'll take full responsibility."

"How?"

"I'll make up something. But let's not borrow trouble."

"If you say so, mate."

Andy grinned. "That accent knocks me out. How long were you Down Under?"

"Almost thirty years."

"Why come back after all that time?"

"Missed my family. And…I met Jo."

"Whoa. You came back for her even though you'd never—"

"That's right."

"Well, she wasted no time inviting you to spend the weekend with her. She must have a similar craving."

"Lucky for me, she seems to. This weekend is critical, though."

"Sounds like tonight is critical."

"I'm not too worried about that part. All we need is uninterrupted time alone. That cabin might be the perfect settin', after all. Peaceful. No distractions."

"Yeah." Andy nodded. "Although—"

"Time for pie!" Ida came in carrying two full-sized plates. Each held a generous wedge of apple pie with vanilla ice cream mounded on top. Tiny waterfalls of melted ice cream ran down the cut sides, curving over protruding apple chunks and pooling at the base.

Brendan grinned. "Now *that's* what I call a piece of pie." He was eager to get to the cabin with

Jo, but dessert like this was worth a short delay. The sensual punch of his first bite was damn near orgasmic.

Halfway through he paused long enough to heap praise on Ida.

She flushed. "I'm glad you like it."

"I don't just *like* it. I plan to nominate it for the Apple Pie Hall of Fame."

"Is there one?"

"If there isn't, I'll see about startin' one. I've had some great pies, but this beats them all. How is it that you're not famous?"

"I thought the same thing," Jo said. "Lots of potential with the canned goods, the pies, the cozy cabin. Speaking of that, did you and Andy get everything sorted out?"

"Pretty much." He looked over at Andy. "What were you sayin' when the pie arrived?"

"Not important. Seth and I will walk over with you with clean linens and such. Normally we'd drive over, but the truck's still loaded with hay and there's no way we'll get all the stuff plus the four of us in the cab. Easier to just hike there."

"I've got sheets, towels and blankets packed in a waterproof bag," Ida said. "Don't forget to take the vacuum when you go down there."

"Planned on it." Andy excused himself from the table and picked up his plate. "Bound to be some dust and cobwebs." He looked at Jo. "Think of this like a beloved vacation home you have to leave for months at a time. Every time you come back, you have to check out what's happened in your absence."

She nodded. "I'm up for that. I don't mind a few cobwebs and a layer of dust."

Brendan was glad to hear it. Truth be told, a rustic cabin was more his speed than a fancy resort, anyway.

12

Before heading out to the cabin, which reportedly would take a few minutes on a path that hadn't been shoveled, Jo accepted rain boots and a thick wool scarf from Ida. Brendan took a little more convincing before he agreed to switch his cowboy boots for the mukluks Andy loaned him.

Ida stuffed newspapers in their leather boots and tucked them in a canvas drawstring bag. "Now I feel better." She handed the bag to Brendan. "These weren't meant for tromping through deep snow. They're too nice."

"Much obliged," Brendan said. "Jo, want to put your purse in here, too?"

"Sure." She tucked it in with the boots and turned to Ida. "I still think we should stay and help with—"

"Never mind the dishes. The boys will help me when they get back. Get settled before the snow gets worse. You must be exhausted. Time for bed."

Bed. There was a loaded word. Jo managed a quick smile. "That wonderful meal gave me a second wind."

"It was terrific," Brendan said. "Thank you."

"The boys and I whip up a hearty breakfast, too. We eat early, though."

"Just tell us what time and we'll be here," Jo said. "We'll keep to your schedule." If they didn't, Ida was liable to fix a second breakfast just for them. Not having that.

"At six, but—"

"Like my wife said, we'll be here." Brendan glanced at Jo, a gleam in his eye. "Ready?"

"Yep." That sexy gleam said so much. Anticipation curled in her stomach.

Andy pulled on his gloves. "Then let's get you guys down there." He picked up one suitcase, tucked a canister vacuum under his arm and grabbed an industrial-sized flashlight. Seth took the other suitcase and the bag stuffed with sheets, blankets and towels.

Brendan hoisted a snow shovel and a broom over one shoulder and carried the bag containing their boots and her purse. Jo scooped up a pillow under each arm. They looked brand new, still in the original packaging so they were protected from the weather. Ida was pulling out all the stops for them.

"We'll go ahead of you and make a path," Andy said as he went out the door.

"Great." Brendan glanced at her. "We'll be warm and cozy before you know it."

"Right." Warm and cozy in the same bed with a rugged cowboy who looked especially dashing with his coat collar turned up and a shovel and broom balanced on one broad shoulder. Whew. She loosened the wool scarf she'd wrapped around her neck. Bring on the chill wind.

"Watch yourself on the porch steps," Ida said as she held the door open.

"I will, thanks." Jo followed Brendan out. The drop in temperature felt good for a millisecond. After that it poked needles up her nose and made her chest ache. "Damn."

Brendan turned at the bottom of the steps. "Maybe you need an extra layer." His breath fogged the air. "Ida might have—"

"I'll be fine." She tugged the scarf up over her nose and mouth. Better. "Just not used to being outside on a night like this."

He planted the shovel and broom handle in the snow and held out a gloved hand. "I keep forgettin' you're a city girl."

"Town girl." She took his hand as she descended the slippery steps. Snow pelted her, seemingly from all directions. "Does this count as a blizzard?"

"Might." He pulled the shovel and broom out of the snow and braced them on his shoulder again.

"You two okay back there?" Seth called out.

"Yea, yea, we're comin'! Had to get situated!" He lowered his voice. "You set the pace."

"I'll make it brisk." She started off. "Helps keep me warm." She called to Andy and Seth, who stood several yards away, waiting for them. "Go ahead, guys!"

"What's that?" Andy started back toward her.

"She said to keep going!" Brendan's deep voice carried better.

"Don't want to lose you! This is a humdinger of a storm!" Andy turned around and made his way back to Seth. They headed off, plowing ruts through knee-deep snow.

"Humdinger is right," Jo kept her head down and stayed in the path they were forging as they trudged past an old hip-roofed barn. "What do you suppose the temperature is?"

"You don't wanna know."

"Did you have weather like this in Australia?"

"Yes, ma'am." A moment later he started laughing.

"What?"

"Just thinkin' about the champagne I was goin' to order from room service."

"Guess you won't be doing that."

"Guess not."

"There's always tomorrow night."

"Yea, yea, we'll get there. I have confidence in Seth."

"So do I. They're a wonderful family."

"They are. Which reminds me, I wanted to ask Andy somethin'." He raised his voice. "Hey, Andy, since you bought hay you must have critters in that barn."

"Three horses and a milk cow."

"I'll help you feed in the mornin'."

"Nah, you don't need to—"

"I'm used to it. Done it all my life. I'll meet you at the barn at five-thirty."

"Me, too," Jo said.

He glanced at her in surprise.

"I used to help Kendra sometimes. Since I moved to town, I don't get to. I like it."

"Alrighty, then." He peered into the darkness. "I do believe that's the cabin up ahead."

A dark shape became more distinct as they drew closer. "None too soon. My lips are frozen."

"I promise to fix that once our friends leave."

"Aren't yours frozen, too?"

"No, ma'am. I have naturally hot lips."

She laughed, which turned into a cough as cold air invaded her lungs.

"Careful. Don't go hurtin' yourself."

"*Naturally hot lips*. That's a good one."

"I'll prove it shortly."

"Looks like we'll need that shovel," Andy called over his shoulder. The beam of his flashlight swept over the front of a log cabin slightly bigger than a double-car garage. Drifts had piled up on the tiny front porch and blocked the bottom half of the front door.

"I'm on it." Brendan turned to her and lifted the bag that held their boots. "Could you—"

"You bet." She squashed the pillows under her left arm and took charge of the bag.

He handed the broom to Seth before burying the blade of the shovel in the drift. He attacked the mound of snow with a vengeance while she stomped her feet to keep warm. Not

Andy and Seth. They stood unmoving and watched Brendan shovel.

She glanced at them. "How can you guys just stand there? Aren't you cold?"

"We're acclimated," Andy said.

Seth chuckled. "That, and we have a little more meat on our bones than you do. We're acclimated *and* insulated."

She continued to stomp. "I'd be better insulated if I could be lucky enough to eat your mom's cooking all the time. I'm already looking forward to breakfast."

Andy smiled. "I'll tell her that."

"Please do. I wasn't kidding about the potential of your various assets. You just might have a goldmine here."

"Did you really leave your cards at home?"

"Uh, no, but—"

"Thought so. You didn't want Mom to see how your name was on it."

"Right."

"If you'll give me one before you leave, I'll keep it to myself. And I'll be in touch."

"G-good." The stomping was losing its effectiveness and she began to shiver.

"That's good enough, buddy!" Andy called out.

Brendan leaned on the shovel, breathing hard. "Is the door unlocked?"

"Sure is."

"Then let's get the hell inside." Leaning the shovel beside the doorway, he turned the knob and pushed. Then he put his shoulder to the door and pushed again. It broke free. "We're in."

"Flip the light switch on the wall to your left." Andy turned to Jo. "After you."

"Thanks." She hurried up the three steps to the porch and walked through the door. Warmer, but not a whole lot warmer. "Is the h-heat on?"

Andy followed her in and left a suitcase against one wall and shrugged out of his parka. "We set the thermostat at forty-five so the pipes won't freeze."

"F-feels c-colder." The stark overhead light gave her a view of a double bed with a plain wooden headboard. She left the bag of boots by the door and carried the pillows over to the bed.

Not the luxury king she'd envisioned for their first experience, but the mattress looked new. Other furniture included a small wooden dining table with two chairs and one easy chair covered in a faded green and gold pattern near the small fireplace.

Seth closed the door and put down the other suitcase. "Might be a little colder than forty-five in here." He carried the bag of linens over to the bed and set it on the floor. "The grouting between the logs needs to be redone. Likewise around the window. Luckily there's only the one." He gestured to the window on the far side of the bed. "Thermostat's on an inside wall so it's not that accurate."

"Yeah," Andy said. "We can't decide if we should repair the place or tear it down." He tossed his parka onto the easy chair.

"It looks authentic." Brendan glanced around. "Hate to think of you tearin' it down."

"It's authentic, all right." Seth left his parka on the easy chair, too, and picked up the broom. "Mom's great-great grandparents built it." He started sweeping the cobwebs from the rafters. "It's more than a hundred and fifty years old."

"Wow." Jo studied the wall nearest to her. "My friend has an old log cabin on her property. This looks like hers did before she asked one of her sons to seal the spaces between the logs."

"Which is what this place needs." Andy walked into a rudimentary kitchen alcove to the right and adjusted the thermostat. "And another window or two. They were a luxury a hundred and fifty years ago."

The blower came on and the blast of warm air coaxed Jo to take off her coat and scarf. She draped them over the back of one of the wooden chairs. Brrr. She hugged herself.

"Still cold?" Brendan put his coat and hat on top of her stuff.

"Getting warmer by the minute." Especially when he gave her a secret smile.

"There's a little closet next to the bathroom if you want to hang up your coats." Andy came out of the kitchen area and plugged in the vacuum.

"Might as well do that." Brendan scooped up his hat and their coats and carried them into the narrow hallway.

"I'll get out the linens." Jo crossed to the bed and untied the drawstring on the bag as Andy started up the little vacuum, which wheezed and rattled in protest.

Seth came over. "Found the towels yet?"

"Right here."

"I'll take 'em."

She handed them over and searched the bag for the mattress protector. Might as well make the bed. Her stomach quivered.

"Hang on," Andy called over the noise. "Let me vacuum there first."

She shoved everything back in and picked up the bag.

He made a few passes over the mattress before running the vacuum quickly around and under the bed. "It's all yours."

"Thanks." She dug out the quilted pad again and walked around to the far side of the bed.

"I'll help with that."

She met Brendan's warm gaze across the expanse of mattress. *Breathe, girl.* "That would be great." She secured her side and he did the same on his.

Then he searched the bag and came up with the fitted sheet, a green and white leaf pattern. After unfolding it, he shook it so it billowed out over the mattress.

Jo caught her side. Ten seconds later the fitted sheet was on and he brought out the flat one. My, weren't they being calmly efficient. They'd make their bed and then they'd lie in it. Not calmly and efficiently, though. She could guarantee that much.

Andy shut off the vacuum and wound up the cord. "That's it for the vacuuming."

Seth came out of the kitchen. "Bathroom and kitchen are in good shape. There are some tea bags in a canister if you want something hot to drink."

"That might be nice." Jo wasn't in the mood for it now, but maybe later, while she and Brendan were lying in the rosy aftermath of...yeah, no. She wouldn't be in the mood for tea then, either.

"Then I guess we're done." Andy went over to the easy chair and grabbed his parka. "Anything else you need before we take off?"

"Can't think of anythin'." Brendan glanced at her. "You all set?"

"I think so."

Seth zipped his parka and gestured to a large wood bin next to the fireplace. "Enough there for a night or two."

Jo glanced at the generous wood supply. "Will we need it?" The combo of the cabin's heater and making up the bed with Brendan's help had warmed her considerably.

"It's worth building one." Andy flipped up his hood. "There's no damper for the flue, so the cold air comes right down the chimney. A good fire counters that, although the fireplace doesn't draw as well as it should. If it gets too smoky, open the door. I wouldn't touch that window. It's not all that stable."

Open the door? Was he nuts?

Brendan nodded as if that was a logical move. "Good to know. Appreciate all this, mates." He shook hands with each of them.

Although Jo had only been acquainted with these two for a few hours, she gave each of them a quick hug. "Thank you for escorting us down here and for giving the place a cleaning."

They became adorably bashful and mumbled something about being glad to do it.

Andy recovered himself first. "See you in the morning. And seriously, neither one of you need to help us feed."

"We'll be there," Jo said.

Seth beamed at her. "You'll love our cow, Jo."

She laughed. "Can't wait to meet her."

"She's brown and white and sweet as they come. We named her Mumu, not like the sound a cow makes, but after those dresses in Hawaii that are—"

"C'mon, Seth. Grab the broom." Andy picked up the vacuum and headed for the door.

"I was just—"

"I know. They'll meet the critters tomorrow." Andy glanced over his shoulder as he ushered his brother outside. "Call if you need us."

"I will." The second the door closed, Brendan turned toward her. "At last. I was beginning to think—"

A cell phone chimed, the sound muffled. It wasn't hers. She glanced up at him. "Who's that?"

"My brother." He started toward the hallway. "Left my phone in my coat."

"Why would he be calling?"

"Can't imagine. He wouldn't unless it's critical."

He hadn't even made it to his phone before Kendra's ring sounded from the bag where she'd stashed her purse. Something must be seriously wrong. She ran to the bag and managed to get to her phone before it went to voicemail. "Kendra?"

"Oh, my God, are you okay?"

"We're fine, but—"

"We saw the big pileup in the news just now, and when we called the resort you weren't there. We were both frantic. We called both phones because—"

"We're fine, just fine. We didn't get that far, so we weren't involved in that accident, thank God."

"Where are you?"

"It's a long story." She gazed at Brendan, who was talking in a low voice with his brother but looking at her.

Kendra still sounded worried. "Do you have a place to stay?"

"We're in a cozy little cabin and just finished a wonderful meal. We hope to get to the resort tomorrow."

"But what happened?"

"Like I said, it's a long story." As she walked toward the hallway, Brendan came to meet her, his words to Quinn sounding much like hers to Kendra.

She met his gaze. "I'll call you tomorrow and give you the whole scoop. In the meantime, would you please call Mandy and tell her we're okay, but the plan changed?"

"Sure, but—"

"The thing is, we're about to...turn in."

"Oh. Oh! Okay!" Happy laughter. "Hanging up now. Have fun." The line went dead.

Brendan smiled at her. "Yea, yea, bro. No worries. I will." He took the phone from his ear and pressed his thumb to disconnect the call as he eliminated the distance between them, slid his free arm around her and pulled her close. "He told me to have fun."

She trembled with eagerness. "She told me the same thing."

"Think we can manage that?"

"Let's give it our best shot."

<u>13</u>

For a weekend that was supposed to be a slam-dunk, the setup had turned into one complicated rodeo. But the ultimate reward was in sight, and Brendan couldn't wait to claim it.

He still had a few obstacles in his path, like the phone in his hand and the one in Jo's. For what he had in mind, they'd need both hands. But dropping them on the floor was an expensive option.

Exerting gentle pressure, he guided her over to the little table. "Phones down." He laid his on the table.

"Phones down." She put hers next to his. "What next?"

"We could jump straight into bed, but since I haven't had an opportunity to unpack my suitcase…"

"Gotcha. Here's an idea. You rummage through your suitcase for what you need while I strip down and slip between the sheets."

"Then I don't get to undress you."

"An unnecessary obstacle."

"But I'm good at it."

"I have no doubt. You can show off your skills tomorrow night after we get to the resort. For now, let's stick to basics."

"When you're right, you're right. But I need somethin' to carry me through the temporary separation." Leaning down, he captured her mouth and sank into a kiss that riled him up faster than it had any right to do.

Breathing hard, he lifted his head. "You taste like apple pie."

"So do you." Grabbing his head, she pulled him close for another go-round.

If he'd ever enjoyed kissing this much, he couldn't recall it. Jo had an amazing mouth and she knew exactly what to do with it. When she sucked on his tongue...ah, yea. Had to ease up on that. He'd worked hard over the years to hone his control, but she might be able to break him down.

Pulling away from her was tough, but unless he did, he wouldn't gain possession of those little raincoats. With a groan of regret, he broke contact with her oh-so-tasty lips. Releasing his hold on her tempting body took willpower, but at last his mind was clear enough to zero in on his duffle propped next to the front door.

That meant ignoring the delicious rustling and slide of clothing happening over by the bed. He wanted to look, but forced himself not to. He wouldn't be able to look without wanting to touch, and fondle, and kiss, and...

Face it—he was obsessed with Jo Fielding, a business professional who worked in a bank, for God's sake. Created spreadsheets for her own amusement, no doubt. Couldn't explain why he found that sexy, why her self-possessed attitude turned him on, why he was shaking with anticipation as he unpacked the box of condoms.

When he stood up and turned around, her clothes, folded and in a neat pile, sat on the table with her silver hoop earrings on top. He got a quick glimpse of her deliciously naked self before she threw back the sheet and two blankets, dived into the bed and pulled the covers up to her chin.

"Are you feelin' shy? Should I douse the light?"

"I'm f-feeling c-cold. B-but the overhead l-light—"

"Leaves somethin' to be desired." He laid the condom box on top of the blankets and looked around. "No table lamps."

"Nope. Or n-nightstand."

"Sure isn't. Let me see what I can do about the light." He headed for the kitchen. Usually there was a—aha, sure enough, a tube-style fluorescent one was mounted under the cupboard above the sink. He turned it on. Not even slightly romantic, but an improvement over the operating-room effect of the ceiling light.

Walking back to the door, he hit the switch on the wall. The glare was gone, but the bluish glow from the kitchen didn't reach very far. The bed was mostly in shadow. "How's that?"

She chuckled. "Industrial. B-better, though."

Crossing the room again, he picked up one of the wooden chairs on the way, set it next to the bed and transferred the condom box to the chair.

"G-good idea."

"Are you really that cold?" He opened the box and took one out, so it'd be ready when the time came. "'Cause I'm not."

"You're d-dressed."

"And fired up thinkin' about you under those covers."

"There's a d-draft."

"Yea, yea, I feel it." He glanced at the window cut into the log wall on the far side of the bed. "That window's lost most of its caulkin'." Sitting on the chair, he pulled off his boots and socks. "A curtain would help some."

"Yep."

"No worries. I'll have you warmed up in no time."

"C-can't wait, H-hot Lips."

"You know it." He stripped off his clothes as fast as he could, mindful of his hard and aching package. As he hung his clothes over the back of the chair, a cold breeze made him shiver. "You're not kiddin' about that draft." He climbed into bed. "Crikey! The sheets are like ice!"

"T-told you."

"You really are shakin' like a leaf." And if they didn't start sharing body heat, he would be, too. Moving over her, he braced his forearms on either side of her head. The light from the kitchen was just enough to let him see her face.

She was looking straight into his eyes.

He looked right back. "Hi." His heart pounded like a son-of-a-gun as he gently settled his body over hers. Didn't give her his full weight.

Her breasts cushioned his pecs and his happy package fit nicely between her thighs.

"Hi." She wrapped her arms around him and her shaking gradually stopped. "You're warm…and…very glad to see me."

"I was hopin' you'd notice." He took a ragged breath. "You feel…great."

"You, too. Your heart's going really fast."

"It tends to do that when I'm thinkin' about…what I'm thinkin' about."

"Bet I know."

"Bet you do." He leaned down and dropped a kiss on her forehead, then one on each satin cheek.

She let out her breath in a long sigh. "This will be okay."

"Were you worried?" He met her gaze.

"It's been a while." She stroked his back. "I didn't know if I…" She swallowed. "But this feels…right."

"Yep."

"You haven't suited up, though."

"Observant of you."

"Why not?"

"Wanted us to get adjusted to each other first. Wanted to find out a little about you, let you get used to me."

She smiled. "Sounds like gentling a horse."

"Yea, yea, with a couple of big differences."

"Like the fact I'm a woman?"

"For one thing. And you can talk. If I do this…" Dipping his head, he nuzzled behind her ear. "You can say if you love it or hate it."

"You know, I'm not sure. Better do it on the other side."

"Glad to." Pressing his mouth to the tender spot behind her earlobe, he kissed her there and nibbled on her earlobe before raising his head. He glanced at her, eyebrows lifted.

"Still not sure." She sounded breathless. "You need to do it some more. And maybe expand your territory."

"Yes, ma'am." Sweetest invitation ever. He started with her mouth, keeping the pressure light and his hands to himself...for now. Kissing his way along her jaw, he moved to her throat, then her shoulder.

Protecting her from the cold as he explored was a challenge. The draft blowing across the bed was wicked. Finally, he grabbed a handful of covers and pulled them over his head. "Scoot down." He raised up to give her room to maneuver.

"We're getting all the way under?"

"Yep." After she wiggled lower, he moved down, too, and his toes went over the edge of the mattress. The sheet he'd tucked in held tight, though, and the blankets stayed in place.

"Cozy."

"Let's take cozy up a notch." Sliding down a little more, he brushed his mouth over her taut nipple and she trembled. "Cold?"

She gulped. "No."

"Turned on?"

"Yes."

"That's what I'm goin' for." He placed kisses in a circle around that quivering nipple.

Then licked it. Her breathing quickened, and when he finally drew the moist bud into his mouth, she moaned and dug the tips of her fingers into his back.

That moan of pleasure went right to his cock. He'd meant to take it slow this first time, but his bad boy had other ideas. As pressure increased in his groin, he balanced on one arm, rose to his knees and slipped his hand between her silky thighs. Damp...

Her breath hitched. The scent of arousal made his blood pound as she relaxed with a sigh of surrender. Her thighs parted, inviting his caress. He buried his fingers in her slick heat.

She gasped. "Brendan..."

"Hm?" Tamping down his own craving, he stroked rhythmically and she tightened around his fingers.

"I'm...used to you...now. You can get the—ohhh..." She gulped.

"Not yet," he murmured, rubbing his thumb over her clit.

"I guess...not." She began to pant as he picked up the pace. "I...oh, Brendan...*Brendan!*" She arched off the bed and yelled. Beautiful sound. The covers slid back, exposing them to the cold air. Didn't matter now. Her climax kept going and she yelled some more.

His cock was begging him to take action immediately or suffer the consequences. Easing his hand free, he snatched the packet from the chair and ripped it open with his teeth. Thank God for the years of practice that allowed him to put it on one-handed.

The covers were totally off and Jo lay there struggling for breath and gazing at his sheathed cock, her eyes dark with passion. "More."

"That's the plan." He'd never had an ache this fierce, or a hunger that made his ears buzz. Grasping her calves, he leaned down and hooked his shoulders under her knees.

Her eyes widened.

"You okay with this?"

"*Oh*, yeah."

"Thought so." He slid his hands under her tush, lifted her up and sank his grateful cock into her still-quivering channel. *Yes.*

Squeezing his eyes shut, he sucked in air and fought for control. When she made a low, humming sound, he opened his eyes.

She gazed up at him, her mouth curved in a soft smile. "Wonderful." Her core muscles clenched. "Again, please."

"Yes, ma'am." He focused on her expression as he eased back and then thrust forward.

Her eyes widened as her breathing picked up speed. "So good." Her response rippled over his cock.

"Sure is." He moved gently. She didn't need much help from him before she began to quiver and gulp for air.

"Come...with me."

"I will." As if he could help it. Her first spasm ignited the fire he could no longer contain. With a shout of relief, he abandoned himself to the heat, loving her with powerful strokes that brought them both to the brink of the inferno and hurled them over the edge.

When he could see straight, he checked to see how Jo was doing.

Her smile was even brighter than before. She looked pleased with herself and with him. "That was big fun."

He laughed. "It was, wasn't it? I'd say this weekend is lookin' up."

14

Jo's instincts about Brendan as a lover had been dead on. His behavior in public translated almost exactly to his behavior in bed. He was easygoing, confident and imaginative. She couldn't ask for a better partner. Hadn't had a better one, either.

When he left the bed to dispose of the condom, he managed to pull the covers over her and keep a grip on the condom. She added thoughtful and coordinated to his list of good qualities.

Poor guy, he had to be freezing his backside hurrying naked down the hall to the bathroom. Maybe there was a wall heater in there. She snuggled under the covers and thanked her lucky stars she was a woman and didn't have to climb out of bed after making love.

Instead she could bask in the warm afterglow of two amazing orgasms. Despite the rocky start, the weekend could still turn out to be awesome.

Brendan came back and created a chilly draft when he slid under the covers. "Don't touch me. I'm like ice."

"I don't care." She grabbed his hands and held them against her cheeks. Not much different from doing a face plant in a snowbank. "How come you didn't turn on the hot water?"

"I did. Waited for a couple minutes and it was still cold. Finally ditched the program and washed up with cold water."

"But there is hot water, right?"

"Supposed to be. Andy said the tank's small. Short showers in the mornin'."

"I can do that."

"Too bad we can't shower together."

"Yeah. We can save that for the resort." Her cheeks had warmed up where his hands cupped her face, but her nose was chilled. "Does it seem colder in here than when we arrived?"

"Seemed like it when I was runnin' nudie up and down the hall."

She smiled. "As in naked?"

"Yes, ma'am. Picked up that term in 'stralia."

"You were over there a long time. Think you'll miss it?"

"Probably will, sometimes." He brushed his thumbs over her cheekbones. "Might visit now and then. Be glad to take you along."

Her chest tightened. *Too soon.* "Um, well, I—"

"No pressure."

"I know. I just—"

"You need to get used to me. No worries. I get it." Leaning forward, he dropped a quick kiss on her mouth. "I'm checkin' out that thermostat. Can't believe the heat's on." He started to get up.

"Wait." She put a hand on his arm. "Let me check it out. My turn to brave the cold."

"Nah, I'll do it."

"You were just out there."

He turned to her with a grin. "'Cause I'm the one with the donger."

She laughed. "Never heard that one."

"It's my favorite. Be right back." Sitting up, he swung his legs over the bed and yelped. "Floor's like a sheet of ice. Puttin' on socks for this operation." The bed jiggled as he located them and pulled them on. "Better." He walked quickly into the kitchen.

Great view. Broad shoulders, tight buns, narrow hips and strong thighs. The heavy wool socks made her smile.

"Bad news on the heating front, Fielding," he called from the kitchen.

"Give it to me straight, Sawyer."

"Andy set it at sixty-five. The thermostat reads forty-two."

"Damn."

"I'll build us a fire."

"While you're nudie?"

"I'm not that much of a hero. I'll fetch my coat from the closet." He started down the hall.

"Would you please bring mine, too?"

"You don't have to get up."

"Yes, I do. We've moved into a new crisis and I'm sharing it with you." But she'd wait for her coat before she left this warm bed. And her socks.

"Hangers rattled in the closet. "Buildin' a fire is a one-person job."

"True."

"So how do you picture us sharin' the crisis?"

"While you build a fire I'll make us some tea. I think a busted heater calls for hot tea."

"Alrighty. I'm startin' to see the erotic potential of this plan."

"What's erotic about being stuck in a cabin with no central heat?"

"A blazin' fire and you nudie except for this sexy black number." He arrived next to the bed wearing his shearling coat and holding her quilted one.

"And my socks, please. They're in my pile of clothes."

"I'll get 'em."

She sat on the edge of the bed and held her feet up as she put on the chilled, slippery coat. Shearling would have felt a lot better.

Brendan returned with her socks. "I'm thinkin' I'll snag a second pair out of my duffle. Want me to bring your suitcase over?"

"Sure." She tugged on her socks. "Maybe we should just get dressed."

His eyebrows lifted.

"I mean, we'd be warmer if we—"

"Buildin' a fire wasn't the only idea I had for solvin' that problem."

His meaningful look told her exactly what that idea was and her core tightened in response. "The bed's not very close to the fire."

"The easy chair is."

"Oh!" She cleared her throat. "So it is."

His gray eyes sparkled. "I'll fetch your suitcase."

Swinging her legs to work off some tension, she studied the easy chair. How would that work, exactly? If only she'd watched more X-rated movies. She snuck a glance at Brendan, who was crouched next to his duffle. "I've never done it in a chair."

"I figured that from your startled reaction." He stood and picked up her suitcase. "No worries." He brought it over and laid it on the bed. "You'll like it."

"How do you know?"

"It's somethin' new." He sat on the other side of the suitcase and put on his second pair of socks. "Somethin' different."

She stared at him. "And that's why I'll like it?"

"Yea, yea." He flashed her a grin. "I have a notion that's what you like about me." He stood and walked over to the wood box.

Was it? Maybe. He was nothing like Robert. Or any of the guys she'd dated briefly after the divorce. His bold sensuality and Aussie accent set him apart. Because he'd never married, he seemed...undomesticated. That thrilled her on a sexual level. But it also made her wary.

The thud of logs as he stacked them in the fireplace sent her into action. She quickly located a second pair of socks in her suitcase and tugged them on before hurrying into the kitchen.

Once there, she filled the kettle with cold water and set it on the burner. "Stovetop works." Then she turned on the hot water tap and let it run.

"How 'bout the oven?" Brendan struck a match. "That could give us some extra heat."

"I'll check." She stepped over to the wall oven set into a cabinet, twisted the knob to Bake and opened the door. "Nope. Nothing happening."

"Then it's a good thing we have firewood."

"Yep." When the kettle whistled, she poured hot water into a teapot and added the mint-flavored teabags she'd found. Then she tested the temperature of the water running into the sink and turned off the faucet. "Looks like we're SOL for hot water, too."

"Sorry to hear it. I'm not a fan of cold showers."

She rinsed out a couple of mugs she found in the cupboard. "We could heat water on the stove and take sponge baths."

"Now that has possibilities."

She laughed. "Thought you'd like it." The fire popped and crackled as she carried a tray loaded with the mugs and the teapot over to the hearth. Brendan had pulled the easy chair closer to the fire and had brought over another of the dining chairs to serve as a table.

"I'll tell you what I like." He put down the fireplace poker and straightened.

"Let me guess." She set the tray on the chair. "Both of us nudie."

"That, too, but I was goin' to say that I like how you roll with the punches when things get all cattywampus."

"Thanks." She poured the tea and handed him one of the steaming mugs. "I've had lots of practice."

"I'm sure you have." He hoisted the mug. "I appreciate the tea."

"You're welcome." She tested it with her tongue. "Careful. It's hot."

"Just how I like it." He gestured toward the easy chair. "Have a seat."

"And then what?"

His puzzled expression gave way to a smile. "I think we should drink the tea you went to the trouble of makin'. A shame to let it get cold while we're otherwise occupied. Besides, the mug is warmin' my hands." He sipped carefully.

"I see." Her skin flushed, heating up the interior of her coat. She resisted the urge to unbutton it. If he could calmly drink his tea after making a remark like that, so could she. She settled into the chair and took a deep breath before bringing the mug to her lips. Slopping tea all over herself would not be cool.

"This sure tastes good." He took another swallow. "Got used to drinkin' tea Down Under."

"My mother-in-law introduced me to it. She was British."

"Was?"

"She died when Mandy was in grade school. Horrible at the time, but during the divorce, I was glad she wasn't around anymore."

"Do you see him?" His tone was casual, but his gaze was not.

"No."

"Does Mandy?"

"No. He—well, it doesn't matter. Did you have afternoon tea in Australia?"

"Sometimes. Dependin' on the work schedule."

"I'm picturing a bunch of cowboys sitting around with flowered teacups and dainty little sandwiches."

"Most likely chipped mugs and a package of Tim Tam biscuits."

"I've heard of those. Chocolate, right?"

"Right." He took a hefty gulp of tea. "Your ex doesn't know about Mandy's baby, then?"

"He wouldn't care."

"Must be a gold-plated bastard."

"Yes, he is. But I'd rather not go into—"

"I know." Taking one last swallow, he set his mug on the tray. "But I'd count it a personal favor if you would."

She clutched her mug in both hands and gazed up at him. "Why?"

"It's part of your story. Made you the amazin' lady you are."

"Not much to tell." She ducked her head and drank more tea.

"I don't need details." Bracing his hands on the arm of the chair, he leaned down, his voice gentle. "But it had to be a big deal, and I—"

"Okay." She lowered the mug and met his gaze. "When Mandy was in high school, Robert was cheating on me with his secretary. I had no idea until she called to say she was six months pregnant."

Brendan's eyes narrowed. "Bloody hell."

"He'd promised her from the beginning he'd ask for a divorce but he kept stalling, even after she was PG. When I confronted him, he blamed me for not being what he needed."

A low sound rose from Brendan's throat. Almost a growl. "Good thing he doesn't come around." His jaw tightened. "Might get messy."

Masculine fury came off him in waves, stirring her blood. Nothing like a knight in shining armor. "The Whine and Cheese Club wanted to clean his clock."

"No wonder." His jaw tightened and his expression grew fierce. "I wouldn't mind a go at the slimy bastard."

"He's not worth the effort."

"Maybe not, but it would be satisfyin'." He sucked in a breath. "Thanks for tellin' me." He glanced down at the mug in her lap. When he looked up, anger continued to glow in his eyes. But slowly it morphed into heat of a different kind. "You still have tea left." His voice dropped to a murmur. "Want it?"

She swallowed. "I want you."

<u>15</u>

"Then it's time for us to trade places." Setting her mug on the tray, he grasped her hands and drew her to her feet. "But first a kiss to start your engine."

She nestled against him and tilted her face up to his. "My engine's already running, mister."

"Let's test that." Heart pounding, he lowered his head and touched down on her full, mint-flavored lips. They parted, inviting him in. With a groan, he thrust his tongue deep and lost his mind. Her tongue began a slow, erotic dance with his and fire licked his privates, tightening his balls and stiffening his cock.

He pulled back, gasping. "You're drivin' me cr—"

"I know." She tugged him down, angled her head and made love to his mouth.

She got him so worked up he was scared he'd come. A kiss hadn't affected him like that in more than thirty years. Holding her head in both hands, he eased away, panting. "Hell's fire, woman."

She gulped for air. "Told you."

"We need...to get...situated." He took her by the shoulders and reversed their positions. Fetching the condom out of his pocket with one trembling hand, he unbuttoned his coat with the other.

"I'll do that." Breathing fast, she took the condom packet and pushed gently at his bare chest. "Relax and enjoy."

He sank down on the chair, but he didn't relax. Good thing, because she dropped to her knees and wrapped her warm fingers around his rigid cock.

He gritted his teeth. "I'm close." And she'd just brought him closer by kneeling at his feet.

"Thanks for the warning." She tightened her grip around the base of his cock and reached for her tea mug.

"You're drinkin' tea *now*?"

Her lips curved in a seductive smile. "I have ideas, too, you know." She sipped from the mug, and without spilling a drop, slid her mouth over the tip of his bad boy while tightening her hold.

That pressure helped stem the tide, but *holy wombat nuts*. Warm liquid swirled over his most sensitive spot as she hollowed her cheeks and took him in. Every time he was sure he'd lose it, she'd squeeze a little harder. Then she'd take him to the brink again.

He dug his fingers into the upholstered arms of the chair, threw back his head and muttered every swear word he knew. When she swallowed the tea and slowly released him, he said a few choice ones out loud as he fought not to come. More sweet torture followed as she rolled on the condom.

Fabric rustled and he opened his eyes.

She stood before him wearing nothing but her socks. Her skin was flushed, her nipples taut and her breasts quivering with each rapid breath. "Doesn't look so...complicated, after all."

"Nope." He prayed he'd keep it together long enough to make her come, too. "Just..." He paused to clear the huskiness from his throat. "Climb aboard."

Holding his gaze, she slipped her hands under his coat and gripped his shoulders. He steadied her hips as she planted one knee on the seat, rose above him and positioned her other knee.

His thunderous heartbeat drowned out every other sound. "I'll guide you." Cupping her tempting ass, he positioned her directly above the target. He gulped. "Right. There."

Her eyes darkened and her fingers pressed into his shoulder muscles. In one firm motion, she took him up to the hilt. Then she began to shake. "Stay still. I don't...I don't want to come yet."

He dragged in a breath. "Me, either."

"I like this."

"Knew you would." His cock twitched.

"You're moving."

"Involuntarily." Her hot sheath tightened and he sucked in air. "Now you're moving."

"Can't seem to...help it." She leaned forward and brushed her lips over his. Then she moaned softly as her core muscles clenched around him again. "I'm gonna come, Brendan. Can't stop. I'm gonna...ahhh..." She surrendered with a wail.

Her rhythmic contractions destroyed what was left of his control and he erupted. Gripping her with both hands, he thrust upward with a roar, burying himself deeper in her throbbing channel.

She gasped and cried out his name as her shudders blended with his. Glorious. She snuggled against him and he wrapped his unbuttoned coat around her.

"Mm." She laid her head on his shoulder.

"I don't ever want to move."

"Then don't."

"Have to, sometime. Nature of the beast."

"But not yet," she murmured. "You're still—"

"Yep. I've always been slow to deflate. Both a curse and a blessin'."

"Right now it's a blessing." She lifted her head and smiled. "Prolongs the pleasure."

"Happy to oblige." He glanced past her. "But the flames are gettin' low. We don't want the fire to go out."

"Then I'll tend to it while you take care of business." She gave him a warm, open-mouthed kiss before slowly disentangling herself. "Yikes. Cold out here." She grabbed her coat and put it on.

"An excellent reason for havin' more sex." Securing the condom, he stood. "Be right back." Then he made tracks for the bathroom.

Washing up wasn't particularly comfortable, but the cold water took care of any remaining inflation issues. He was drying off with a bath towel when Jo screamed.

Dropping the towel, he raced down the hall, coat flapping. "Jo! Jo, are you—" He skidded to a stop.

She wasn't on fire. Instead she clutched her coat with bloodless fingers and stared at the window beyond the bed, her eyes wide with terror.

He glanced in that direction and took a step back. "*Holy crap.*"

"Wh-what is it?"

He moved closer to Jo, putting himself between the thing and her. It was outside and the walls were made of sturdy logs, but still. "I…um…it has horns."

"I *see* that."

"Not elk or moose horns, though." What the fuck was it? A monster from the depths of Hell? But he hadn't believed in monsters for a very long time. Big sucker, though, tall enough to peer in the window with its beady eyes. Shaggy, bearded face matted with snow. Leathery nostrils. Okay. Monster identified. "It's a buffalo."

"A *buffalo*?"

"Yea, yea. That's what it is. Or bison. That's more accurate, but I like the word buffalo better." Figuring out what he was looking at slowed his pulse some, but having a two-thousand-pound wild animal standing outside the cabin was disconcerting.

"Don't they travel in herds?"

"They do."

"We could be surrounded."

"We could. No worries. They likely won't be here long."

"Do you know anything about their habits?"

"Not really. Don't have 'em in 'stralia. Didn't learn much about 'em when I was a kid, either."

"Then how do you know how long they'll hang around?"

He gave her a sheepish smile. "I don't. Just tryin' to calm you."

"By making stuff up."

"Stuff that could be true."

She laughed. "Or not. It's okay. I'm not as scared as I was, but I don't like the way he's looking at us. Would he try to force his way in?"

"I doubt it."

"But you really don't know."

"Not exactly. I'm calling Andy. He needs to hear about this." Keeping an eye on the buffalo, he walked over to the table where he'd left his phone.

"Would you please bring mine?"

"To call Kendra?"

"No. It's late and she'd just worry. I want to look up these critters to see what we're dealing with."

"Good plan."

"One thing's for sure. He's not the least bit afraid of us or he would have taken off when I let out that blood-curdling scream. Just so you know, that's not like me."

"I believe you." He smiled. "No worries. I came close to screamin', too." He held up his phone. "I'll put Andy on speaker so you can hear what he says."

"Great."

Andy didn't answer right away, and when he did, he sounded half-asleep. "What's up?"

"A buffalo's staring in our window. Big one."

"Damn."

Brendan frowned. "You don't sound surprised."

"I was hoping they wouldn't show up."

"But you knew they might?" Brendan glanced at Jo and mouthed *what the hell*. "You should've warned us, mate!"

"They're migratory. They used to come through here every year, but they haven't the last couple of winters."

"Well, they're here, now. Not to be ungrateful, but they scared the shit out of us."

"Oh, man, I hope you weren't right in the middle of—"

"We weren't." And he shouldn't have put this call on speaker.

"So you'd already—"

He ducked his head. "Yea, yea. No worries."

"Whew. I'm glad you were done with that. That's one reason I didn't tell you."

"*What?*"

"You know, this being your first time with Jo and all. You needed to concentrate on what you were doing instead of worrying you might get interrupted by a herd of buffalo."

Jo clapped a hand over her mouth and her shoulders began to shake.

"Appreciate the consideration." Brendan rolled his eyes. Thank God Jo thought it was funny.

"How'd it go?"

Jo put both hands over her mouth but a snort escaped, anyway.

"Fine. About the buf—"

"Congratulations, dude! Sometimes the first go-round isn't all that great. But that could be just me and my inexperience. You, though, clearly have a lot of—"

"What are we supposed to do about the buffalo?"

"Not much you can do. Wait for them to leave."

"How soon will that be?"

"Hard to say. Sometimes hours, sometimes days."

"We're not waitin' days, mate."

"Probably won't have to. They'll likely be gone by morning."

"Hope so. That big bull just backed off a little. Is there any chance he's a loner?"

"Doubt it. We've had anywhere from ten to fifty show up."

"Crikey."

"Before I forget, if they don't leave in the morning, you have food. We stored some of Mom's canned goods on the top shelf of the hall closet when we ran out of room in the house. Help yourself if you can't make it to breakfast."

Brendan exhaled and prayed for patience. "What if we quietly walk out of the cabin and hike back to your house?"

"I wouldn't advise it, dude. They're not docile like cattle. I think they hold a grudge because our forefathers tried to exterminate them."

"Could you fetch us in the truck, then?"

"Tried herding those critters with the truck last time they were here. Never again. If they feel the least bit threatened, they'll either mow you down or gore you. They can run thirty-five miles an hour. If they have a calf, they're even more dangerous."

"But it's winter. They wouldn't have—"

"Oh, yes, they could. They did the time we tried to herd them. Chances are there's a calf or two out there. Don't mess with them. Not worth it."

"Will they come down by you?"

"Never have, but I'll be on the lookout in the morning. For some reason, they gravitate to the area around the cabin. Could be an ancestral thing, for all I know."

"Lucky us." That sounded snarky. "Not that I don't appreciate havin' a roof over our head." Even if that roof was surrounded by a herd of buffalo.

"It might not be ideal, but look on the bright side."

"I'm not losin' sight of that. We could still be in that ditch with no way of gettin' out."

"And so what if the buffalo herd keeps you pinned down for a while? Gives you more time to fool around. Have fun." Andy disconnected.

<u>16</u>

Brendan was adorable when he was embarrassed. Jo couldn't resist teasing him, either. "What exactly did you and Andy talk about when I was in the kitchen with Seth and Ida?"

"It wasn't like he made it sound." He rubbed the back of his neck.

"And how was that?"

"Like I'd mouthed off about us havin' sex for the first time tonight."

"Then how did he know?"

"He asked me if you'd mind a little dust and if your place was neat as a pin."

"What did you say?"

"I had to admit I'd never been in your condo. One thing led to another and he figured out this was our first night together. He just wanted it to be nice."

"Which it was. Is."

"Except we may be trapped here for the whole weekend. We're at the whim of those critters."

"You don't like that, do you?"

"Not much. I was relieved that we had a place to stay and hopeful Seth could fix my truck.

But fixin' my truck won't matter if we can't get to it." He buttoned his coat and tucked his phone in his pocket before walking toward the window. "Maybe Andy's wrong and there's only the one lonesome bull out there."

"Can you tell?" She stayed where she was, unwilling to come face-to-face with that giant creature again. Let Brendan gaze into the darkness. The shock of seeing a scary monster in the window hadn't worn off yet.

Cupping his hands around his face, he peered outside. "Oh, I can tell, all right, even though it's still snowin' like the devil. We're not leavin' until they decide to." He sounded frustrated.

"So not a loner?"

"Not even close. There's at least twenty of 'em out there. One is smaller than the rest. Probably a calf."

"What are they doing?"

"Looks like they're settlin' in for the night."

"Then maybe we should do the same." During the call to Andy she'd buttoned her coat. Not that he could have seen her, but psychologically she'd wanted to be halfway decent for that conversation. Laying her phone on the easy chair, she undid the buttons. "It's not like we're going anywhere now, anyway."

"That's for damned sure." He turned away from the window, clearly irritated by the situation. Then he paused and his breath caught. "I'm an idiot for complainin'." He tossed his phone on the table and started toward her. "Any guy would thank his lucky stars if he could be stranded with you."

The heat in his gaze sent moisture straight to her lady parts. "You're a sweet-talking man, Brendan Sawyer."

"You're a sweet-lovin' woman, Jo Fielding." He spared a quick glance for the fire. "You got that goin' real good." He slipped his hands inside her coat, circled her waist and drew her close. "What do you say we go back to bed?"

"Who'll tend the fire?"

"I will. Right after I tend to you." Cupping her bottom, he picked her up.

"Whoa. Wasn't expecting to be carried there." She wrapped her legs around his hips.

"Just showin' off." He turned and made for the bed. "I've heard women like the strong, silent type."

"You're strong, but I wouldn't call you silent."

He grinned. "Nah, I struggle with that part of the equation." He laid her on the rumpled covers. "I'm leavin' your coat on so you don't freeze your tushy on the cold sheets."

"Thanks." A frigid wind whistled through the gaps between the logs and she pulled her coat closed with a shiver. "Hurry."

"Goin' fast as I can." He unbuttoned his coat and grabbed a condom from the chair he'd left beside the bed. A glimpse of his broad chest and stiff cock sent a message straight to her aching core. She moaned.

"Love that sound." He rolled on the condom and put a knee on the mattress. "Means you want me."

"I think you know that."

"Maybe I do." He moved over her. "Like bein' reminded of it with those sexy little moans, though."

The fleece-lined lapels of his coat draped protectively around her, cocooning her body in a world where nothing else mattered but this intimate connection. The light from the stove was just enough for her to see the hunger in his expression.

Reaching between her thighs, he tunneled his fingers through her damp curls and sighed. "Ah, Jo. So wet, so hot. Makes me feel like a king."

"Involuntary reaction, your highness."

"That makes it even more special." He slid two fingers into her slick channel, curving them to caress her G-spot. "You can't help wantin' me."

She gasped. "Guess not."

"Come for me, pretty lady." He stroked her, his knowing touch coaxing her to surrender now...*now.* She rushed to meet the pleasure, lifting her hips, greeting the waves of release with cries of delight.

"Like that?" His voice was soft and rich with satisfaction.

She dragged in air. "*Oh,* yeah."

"Then let's do it again." Easing his fingers free, he replaced them with the firm thrust of his cock. Then he began to move.

The tantalizing friction took her breath away. Splaying her fingers over his tight ass, she absorbed the rhythmic flex of his muscles as he plunged in again and again, winding the spring ever tighter.

"Wrap your legs around me." His voice was hoarse with strain as he pumped faster. "I want..." He groaned as she granted his request, allowing him to bury his cock even deeper. "Like that...so good, so damn..." His breath hitched. "You're goin' to come. I felt the first..."

She gulped and began to pant. "Yes, I am....yes, *yes!*" Her world exploded.

He drove in once more with a choked cry and shuddered in the grip of his own climax. Braced above her, chest heaving, he gazed at her in wonder. "Incredible."

"Uh-huh."

"I hope I brought enough condoms."

That made her giggle. "It's the newness. We'll slow down soon."

"Speak for yourself, lady. I'm just gettin' started." He gave her a quick kiss before easing away from her. "I'll take my necessary stroll down the hall and then build up the fire. After that I'll be back for more."

"Aren't you sleepy?"

"Are you kiddin' me? I'm in a cold cabin with a hot woman. That calls for action, not sleepin'." He left the bed. "Unless that was a hint that you're sleepy."

"A little bit. I'm—" The glow from the kitchen disappeared, leaving them with only firelight. "Uh-oh."

"Maybe the bulb gave out."

She sat up. "I'll go see."

"No point in both of us runnin' around freezin' to death. If the one in the bathroom works, we're okay." He headed off.

She turned her head and waited for a light to glow from the hallway. Still pitch black, even after he'd had plenty of time to flip a switch.

Brendan muttered an earthy swear word. "Electricity's out, but at least the water's running. They must have a back-up generator for the water pump and the main house."

"So you think they have power?"

"Probably. Doesn't do us much good with a buffalo herd standing guard outside our door. When's the last time you charged your phone?"

"Lunchtime." She climbed out of bed and buttoned her coat. "How about you?"

"Couldn't say for sure," he called over the sound of running water. "I was a little distracted today and I...*iyiyi!* That's *cold.* So much for our warm sponge bath."

"Maybe we can heat up water over the fire."

"That's tricky unless the fireplace is set up for it. You really need cast iron cookware, too."

She located her phone on the easy chair. "My battery's at twenty-eight percent."

"Better turn it off, then."

"Doing it now." The fire gave her just enough light to navigate back to the table. She set her phone next to her pile of clothes.

He came from the hall, buttoning his coat on the way. "I hope to hell I have more room on mine." Picking it up from the table, he tapped the screen, illuminating his face. His beard, a mixture of gray and brown, had started to grow, darkening his chin.

She'd only seen him clean-shaven. This rougher, unkempt version of Brendan looked even less domesticated. Desire curled in her belly.

"My battery's at thirty-six." He powered it down. "We'll have to ration what battery life we have."

"I promised Kendra I'd call her in the morning." She didn't want to. Isolation with this lusty man had freed up a side of her she'd buried for years. Ending the isolation, even with a phone call, might break the spell.

"Maybe we'll have electricity by then."

She sighed. "I have to call her whether we do or not. Otherwise she'll worry."

"Yea, yea, you're right." He reached over and stroked her cheek. "Doesn't seem like you want to, though." He sounded amused.

"Have you ever been in the mood where you don't want to think, just feel?"

"I have." He cupped her face and moved closer. "Quite recently. Gettin' in that kind of mood now."

"Then let's pile some covers and pillows on the floor in front of the fire and get nudie."

17

"Best suggestion ever." Brendan had missed the visual stimulation of Jo's beautiful body in the throes of passion. Building up the fire would provide enough heat to ditch the jackets and enough light to see…everything. "Should we just haul the mattress over, too?"

"I thought of that, but I'm sure there's soot on the floor. They can wash the bedding, but if we get the mattress dirty, that makes a bigger problem for them."

"Good point. I'll take care of the fire if you'll bring over the bedding. And the condoms."

"You have a deal. Meet you there."

He returned to the hearth and checked the supply of wood in the large bin next to it. Andy and Seth had stocked in quite a bit, enough to make it through another day and even another night if necessary.

Before adding logs to the fire, he crouched down and peered into the firebox. An iron hook hung from a bar positioned partway up the chimney. That was a start. He'd beefed up the fire and replaced the screen by the time Jo arrived, her arms full of sheets, blankets and pillows.

She glanced around. "The best spot is where the chair is."

"I'll move it." Picking it up, he set it down several feet away. Then he helped her arrange their makeshift bed. "There's a hook inside the fireplace, so if there's a cast iron kettle in the cupboard, we can heat water. And food, too, for that matter."

"That sounds kind of fun." She put two pillows at one end of the blanket bed.

"Not half as much fun as I plan to have makin' out in front of the fire. Did you remember the—"

"Of course I did." She pulled the box of condoms out of her coat pocket. "Catch."

He snagged them one-handed and put the box on the floor within easy reach.

"I don't know how you do it."

He glanced up. "Do what?"

"Make every move look sexy as hell. It's like long-range foreplay."

"Really?" That brought a big ol' smile to his face. "'Cause I'm not tryin' to achieve such a thing, but if my actions affect you that way, great."

"There's something so effortlessly competent about you. Like just now, catching the box in one hand. When you did that, I felt a zing."

"Oh?" She was too far away. He walked around the blanket bed so he was standing right in front of her. "Where exactly did you feel this zing?"

"Take a guess."

"Might require a few tries." Moving closer, he traced the outline of her mouth with his forefinger. "Here?"

Her eyes sparkled in the firelight. "No."

Undoing the top button of her coat, he brushed his knuckles over the hollow of her throat. "How 'bout here?"

"Nope."

He unfastened another button and slipped his hand inside her coat to fondle her left breast. "Has to be here." He laid his palm flat and gazed into her eyes. "I can feel your heart. Goin' pretty fast, too."

She swallowed. "You make my heart beat faster, but that's not the same as a zing."

"Hm." Working two more buttons loose, he placed his hand against her stomach. "Here?"

"No, that flutters." Her eyes darkened and she sucked in a breath. "But you're getting warmer."

"That's the truth." He stopped working on her buttons, stepped back and undid his. "Between this guessin' game and the fire, I'm startin' to sweat." Taking off his coat, he tossed it in the general direction of the chair.

"See, that's what I mean. You hit the target without looking. And now you're standing there naked, aroused, and...supremely confident."

He smiled and reached for the last button on her coat. "Did I score another zing?"

"A bunch of them."

"Was it here?" He cupped the soft triangle of curls at the top of her thighs.

"As if you didn't know."

"Guessin' games are no fun if you get the answer first thing." Sliding an arm around her waist, he steadied her as he gently stroked the moist entrance that held the key to so much pleasure, his and hers. "Did I win?"

"Uh-huh."

Trailing his damp fingers up her body, he brushed them over her mouth. "What's my prize?"

"I think you know that, too." Her eyes took on a sultry glow as she ran her tongue over her lips. "Your wish is my command."

His breath caught. "I just felt a zing."

"Then you already know what you—"

"Oh, yea, I know what I want. We'll start by gettin' rid of this so I can just look at you." He slipped the coat off her shoulders and sent it sailing toward the chair. It amused him that such things turned her on. At some point, he'd explain where he'd learned those skills.

Not now. This moment was for stepping back and soaking up the wonder of Jo. Firelight danced over her lithe, womanly body. She met his gaze and drew in a ragged breath. Her rose-tipped breasts quivered, making his mouth water.

He looked his fill, absorbing the elegance in the way she held herself, the suppleness suggested by her slim waist and the lean muscles in her toned thighs. "You're magnificent."

She flushed. "Thank you."

"I'm the one who should be doin' the thankin'." He stepped toward her. "Without knowin' much about me, you invited me to spend the weekend with you. I'm still askin' myself how I got so lucky."

"You said it yourself." She reached for him, cupping his face in both hands. "You're different from the men I've known. I like different."

He pulled her close, relishing the press of her breasts against his pecs and her belly against his cock. "Bet you're not crazy about an unshaven man, though."

"You know what? Normally I'm not." She ran her thumbs over his beard. "But I like you this way. Gives you a roguish look."

"I'm not a rogue." He massaged the small of her back and breathed in the scent of her. She wore something tangy, like citrus, but arousal was mixed in there, making the aroma damned near irresistible.

She smiled. "I think maybe you are a rogue."

"No, ma'am."

"If you say so."

"I do." If her assessment bugged him a little, he'd let that go, too. "And to prove it, I'm goin' to make sure I don't give you beard burn."

"It's okay if you do." She caressed his bristly face. "I mean, if you get carried away and forget."

"Would I do that?" Yea, yea, he might, especially when she looked at him as if she could eat him up with a spoon. She could turn him into a wild man in no time. "I have an idea."

She wiggled against him. "I know."

"Beyond that. How 'bout if I take the bottom this time? That way I'm not as likely to ravish your face."

"So I'll be in charge?"

"That's usually how it works."

"I'm in." Scooting out of his arms, she walked around him, leaned down and threw back the top layer of blankets to expose the sheet underneath. "Go ahead and lie down."

"First I'll put another log on the—"

"I'll do it." Her gaze swept over him and lingered on his jutting cock. "I'll handle...everything."

She was acting bossy as hell and he loved it. While she set aside the screen and added another piece of wood to the fire, he stretched out on his back. The wooden floor under the blankets didn't have much give to it, so even better that he'd be cushioning her instead of the other way around.

By turning his head, he could see her tending the fire while she was nudie. How he loved the shape of her ass. And the graceful curve of her spine as she leaned over to rearrange chunks of burning wood with metal tongs.

She'd embraced his suggestion for this interlude, but next time maybe she'd go for making love doggie style. And the time after that, they could...*cool it, Sawyer*! If he didn't, she might think sex was all he cared about. She might already think that.

Oh, he cared a lot about it, but only because he was having it with her. He'd talked with his Goondeen for hours about whether he'd ever find a woman who affected him like this, a woman he longed to be with for the rest of his days.

Well, he'd found Jo and had told his Goondeen about her, or as much as he'd known at the time. His Goondeen had warned him to be patient, to let the relationship develop gradually. So much for that possibility. Nothing gradual about this weekend.

Jo replaced the screen, turned and walked the short distance to their blanket bed. "That should do it for now." She dropped to her knees beside him. "Evidently you haven't lost interest."

"Watchin' you tend the fire did the trick. I've fallen in love with your ass."

"I'm rather enamored of yours, too." She slid a bare knee over his abs and then settled her tush on his stomach only a short distance from his aching bad boy. "The rest of you also works for me." She placed her hands on his pecs and spread her fingers. "Just the right amount of chest hair. Manly but not overwhelming."

"Glad you approve." His cock twitched with impatience. "Not to rush you, but there's a critical problem developin' right behind you."

She nodded. "I'm aware."

"Are you familiar with the term *blue balls*?"

"I am. Always wondered if it was literal. Do they really turn—"

"No, but believe me, it feels like they do."

"Can't have that." Rising to her knees, she scooted backward and settled on his thighs. "Help is on the way." She reached for the box of condoms and in less than thirty seconds had him suited up.

Quick as she'd been while doing it, he'd almost come...twice. Having her fool with his cock while her breasts quivered enticingly was almost more than a man could be expected to withstand.

But he'd managed and now his reward was at hand.

Bracing her hands on his chest, she eased down, taking him in slowly, which was fine with him. Speed might have set him off.

When she was fully anchored, she leaned forward until her nipples brushed his chest. "How're you doing?"

"Spectacular." He stroked her back. "Couldn't be better."

"Your voice is a little raspy."

"Yours, too." He dragged in a breath, expanding his chest to create more contact. "Feels good when you rub against me."

"Feels good to me, too." She slid forward and back, teasing him with her breasts while creating subtle friction lower down.

"Mm." He bracketed her hips. "More of that, please."

"Your wish is my command."

"I think we both know who's in command of this operation."

Her answering smile confirmed it as she propped herself up a little more so she had enough leverage to create a smooth, steady rhythm. "Is that working for you?"

"Workin' a little too well." He sucked in a breath. "How 'bout you?"

"I'm just hanging out, having fun watching you get wound up."

"Hey, no fair."

"Sure it is. You get to be the all-powerful one who holds it together while I come apart. My turn to make you come first."

"That's not how it's supposed to—"

"Who says?"

"Me." He gasped as she picked up the pace. "If I come, then you might not. Slow down."

"Nope. You're toast, mister." Sitting back, she rode him hard.

He'd wanted a visual. Holy hell, he had all a man could ask for as she slid up and down his happy cock, her breasts quivering and her flushed skin bathed in firelight.

He came, whether he intended to or not, and likely gave her a show, too. He wailed like a banshee and likely swore a fair bit judging from the way she was grinning at him when the red haze of lust cleared enough for him to focus.

His throat was raw and his voice a mere croak. "What about you?"

"No problem." Still anchored securely to him, she slipped her hand between her thighs. Within seconds she let out a triumphant cry as she came.

Because they were still linked, he experienced her climax, too. Usually at this moment he was dealing with his own intense needs. This time he could savor her reaction to pleasure. The afterglow of her release filled him with tenderness.

He held out his arms. "Come here."

She collapsed against his chest and laid her head on his shoulder as she gulped for air.

Wrapping his arms around her, he leaned over and kissed her gently on the forehead. "Thank you."

"Welcome."

"I don't think I've ever come that hard."

"Good."

"Watching you come afterward was amazin', too. Gave me a whole new appreciation for how beautiful that moment is."

She took a deep breath and let it out. "Your moment is beautiful, too."

"Even when I'm swearin'?"

"That's kind of funny."

He rested his cheek on the top of her head. "Australians, at least the ones I hung out with, swear a lot. I got in the habit."

"I noticed. You went bonkers for a while, there."

"Which was all your fault."

"Sure was. I like being in charge of you."

"Anytime." His instinctive response startled him. It came from a place he was only beginning to access.

"I doubt that." She lifted her head and propped it on her chin so she could look at him. "Letting me drive your truck is one thing, but you're not the kind of guy who turns over—"

"Anytime, Jo." He held her gaze.

She was staring at him as if she thought that was a lot of hooey, but no worries. He understood why she'd pegged him as a certain type. He just hoped the new version would excite her as much as the rogue she thought he was.

<u>18</u>

Sleeping on the floor wasn't optimal, but Jo agreed with Brendan that having the fireplace next to them made it a better choice than the bed. She was exhausted enough that she could probably conk out anywhere.

Brendan insisted she take the spot closest to the fire and he spooned her to keep her back warm. He kissed the tip of her ear. "I still want you, but I'm lockin' that down. We need sleep."

"We do." She chuckled. "But you're not quite locked down."

"I'm workin' on it. At least I'm not as hard as the floor."

"Not yet."

"You know what? Sleepin' on the floor is silly. We should drag the mattress over here. If it gets ruined, I'd be happy to buy them a new one."

"They'd never accept it."

He sighed. "No, they wouldn't. They'd be insulted by the offer. What the heck. It's only for what's left of tonight."

"What time do you think it is?"

"I know what time it is. Almost three-thirty."

"How do you know that?"

He tucked her in closer. "I could pretend I learned ninja time-tellin' skills from my Goondeen."

"But you didn't?"

"Never got the hang of it. My watch is over on the chair by the bed. I checked it when I disposed of that last condom."

"I forgot all about your watch."

"I didn't think it would add anythin' to our first time between the sheets, so I took it off."

"Does it do anything special?"

"It tells time with pinpoint accuracy. That's special."

"I mean does it connect to the Internet?"

"It does not. That's what I love about it. I wanted the kind you can wind, but those are scarcer than hen's teeth. This one has hands and numbers like I wanted, but it runs on a battery. The only time it fails me is when the battery gets weak."

"But if it was one of those digital watches with an Internet connection, we could—"

"If it was that kind of watch, the fellow with his hand cupping your breast wouldn't be me."

"Are you anti-technology?"

"I have a smartphone. I just don't need to be wearin' it all the time. Which begs the question—why don't you have one of those super-duper watches?"

"My phone's good enough. I don't want to wear a computer on my wrist, either. I've just been evaluating our resources and wondered if we have any untapped ones."

He nibbled on her earlobe. "I love it when you talk like a banker."

"That's banker talk?"

"Yes, ma'am. I'd say *reviewin' our options.* You say *evaluatin' our resources.* It turns me on, especially when you're nudie."

"Why?"

"In your office, you're all efficiency and control. But you can totally lose it when I'm lovin' you." He squeezed her breast and flicked his thumb over her nipple. "I know your secret self, and she's hot stuff."

Desire bubbled up inside her. "I thought we were going to get some rest."

"I thought so, too." He gave her breast one last caress and moved his hand between her thighs. "But it seems someone's all juiced up and ready to go."

"This is crazy." But he'd learned exactly how she liked to be touched and he was using that knowledge to great effect.

"You don't have to do a thing. I'll handle this."

"You'll be in charge of me?"

"If that's okay with you." His voice held a note of hesitation.

"It's okay with me." As if she'd say no to him. She was wide awake and craving whatever he had in mind.

He rolled away from her and foil crinkled as he opened another condom packet. Then he was back, adjusting her position, tilting her hips, and sliding his sheathed cock effortlessly into her wet and aching core.

He thrust once, deepening the connection, and she sighed. "I can't believe how much I wanted you to do this."

"You did?"

"I thought of it when we settled in to go to sleep."

"You should have said so." He stroked slowly and deliberately. "Your wish is my command."

"But…" Her breath hitched as the spring tightened within her. "We should be sleeping."

"We will. After this. It won't take long."

"No. I'm super relaxed, yet…"

"So ready."

"Uh-huh."

"Let it happen. Let go."

She did, moaning softly with pleasure. No fireworks this time. Only a lovely, sweet release of tension.

"Perfect." Brendan's murmured word was followed by a gasp and a shudder as he came, too. He held her close until the quivering stopped and she released a long, slow breath.

He was the best, most sensitive lover she'd ever had. Lulled by a gentle orgasm that readied her for sleep, she drifted in a haze of pleasure.

A waft of cold air meant he'd left to dispose of the condom. Warm arms gathering her close told her he was back. She slept.

Sometime later, the crackle of the fire woke her. Pale light spilled through the window, allowing her to see the interior of the cabin, but she couldn't guess the time. A snowdrift blocked part of her view, but flakes still swirled in the wind.

Brendan had put on his jeans as well as his coat, which made sense because the tip of her nose was *freezing.* In her sleep, she'd pulled the covers over every other part of her face, but she had to breathe. "Are the buffalo still out there?"

He glanced over his shoulder. His hair was rumpled and his beard had filled in even more. He looked like a mountain man stoking up the campfire. "Yes, ma'am, they are. Mornin', sunshine."

"Morning, cowboy."

He chuckled. "That's *jackaroo,* thank you very much."

"I gather that's an important distinction."

"You bet your sweet ass it is."

She sat up, pulled the blanket around her shoulders, and took a closer look at the fire. "You found a cast iron kettle!"

"I did. And I'm heatin' water in it. Your choice. Should I use it for tea or shavin' off my whiskers?"

"Tea. I like your beard. You should let it grow."

"I'll take that under advisement."

"I hate to give up these cozy covers, but..."

"Nature calls. Let me warm your coat in front of the fire. That'll help." He went over to the chair and fetched it. Then he walked back and held it near the fireplace.

"Too bad nobody was awake to do the same for you."

"The lining of mine doesn't get chilled like yours does. Okay, that should do it. Don't want to melt the material." He held it for her.

She stood quickly and shoved her arms into the sleeves. "Ah, that's great." She buttoned it and turned. "You're a lifesaver."

"I'd rather be a piece of Godiva chocolate."

She laughed. "If you were candy, you'd definitely be Godiva. Decadent, tempting and extremely satisfying."

"Thank you. Good to know last night wasn't some male fantasy I conjured in my sleep."

"Nope." She gave him a quick kiss and tasted mint. "You brushed your teeth!"

"Seemed like the thing to do."

"I'm brushing mine, too." She hurried over to her suitcase and pulled out her toiletries bag. "Get ready to be kissed with vigor."

"Not before I shave."

"That's what you think." She headed for the bathroom. Although she was touched that he was determined not to give her a rash, she was totally against shaving off his beard. He already had a great start on it. Soon it would be silky instead of prickly. Maybe not before the weekend was over, but by next week.

And yes, she'd taken that mental leap. She wanted to keep seeing him after this weekend. She had no illusions that they were building something permanent. Any guy who'd gone this long without making a commitment wasn't a prime candidate for a long-lasting relationship. That was fine with her.

More than fine. Until meeting Brendan she hadn't figured out that a fascinating, untamed rogue was exactly the kind of man she needed. He clearly wasn't enamored of marriage and after the disaster with Robert, neither was she.

A few minutes later she returned to the living room. Flames leaped in the fireplace and Brendan had set two mugs and a teapot on the dining chair he'd brought over by the hearth the night before.

"This all looks so cozy."

"It does, but the wood's goin' faster than I estimated. I didn't factor in how much more we'd use between midnight and seven compared to what we'd burned from seven to midnight."

She peered into the wood box. "I see what you mean."

"At this rate, we'll run out by this afternoon."

"Maybe the buffalo will decide to leave before then."

"Doesn't look like it. They'd be gettin' restless, start millin' around if they were ready to head out. Instead they're bedded down on the leeward side of the house." He poured their tea and handed her a mug.

"Thanks." She took a restorative sip. "You can see all that from the window?"

"I went out on the porch."

Her eyes widened. "When?"

"While you were in the bathroom. Wanted to test whether they'd take any notice of me."

She glanced toward the door. His borrowed snow boots were there with water beaded on the rubbery surface. He'd walked right out that door despite Andy's warning. "What if one of them had come after you?"

"I kept my eye on them. I would have scooted back inside if they'd shown any sign of aggression."

"Hm."

"I can move damned fast when I have to."

"So can they. What Andy told you is the same thing I'd found on the Internet. People have been gored because they underestimated the speed of those animals."

He swallowed a mouthful of tea. "I'm not underestimatin' them. But I watched them for a bit. Got a sense of their mood. I could likely walk back to the house, load up on wood and walk back without stirrin' up those critters at all."

Her stomach hollowed out. "Or you could be trampled to death." She gazed at him over the rim of her mug. "Please tell me you're not considering that."

He shrugged. "We need the wood."

"We can ration it. Put on more clothes."

"And start burnin' the furniture?"

"I'd rather do that than have you risk your life getting more wood."

"I wouldn't be riskin' my life. Like I said, I got a sense of their mood. They're mellow right now."

"You don't know that!"

"As a matter of fact, I do."

"Were you even listening to Andy? You may be able to read cattle and horses after being around them so much, but these creatures are wild. And huge."

"Just because they're wild doesn't mean they're unpredictable."

Panic rose in her chest. "Of course it does. That's why it can go bad when people try to keep wild animals as house pets. The wildness is still there, making them unpredictable. That's common knowledge."

He drained his mug and set it back on the chair. "I'm not plannin' to make those critters into pets. I respect them but I don't fear them. They startled me at first, but now that I've had a chance to observe them, I get who they are."

She frowned. "*Who they are*?"

"I didn't learn how to intuitively tell time when I studied with my Goondeen, but I kicked butt when it came to communicatin' with animals."

"Wild animals?"

"Wild or tame. Doesn't matter. Just now, when I went out on the porch, I put out mental feelers and identified the dominant male. We watched each other for a while. He knows I'm not a threat."

A chill zipped up her spine. "And you think you can walk among them without getting hurt? I've read about guys who think that. One was killed by the bears he thought were his friends."

"I read about him, too. Not my intention at all. I'm not tryin' to be part of their routine. I just want to do my thing and let them do theirs. Big difference."

"Brendan, don't go out there." She put down her unfinished tea, walked over and gripped the front of his coat. "Don't take such a ridiculous risk. We'll figure out some way around the wood shortage."

He framed her face in his warm hands. "I've thought it through and this makes the most sense. I'm trained for it. Andy and Seth aren't, so they're scared and probably should be if they don't know what they're doin'. I sure as hell wouldn't want them trying this."

"But they wouldn't."

"I'm not so sure. Come to think of it, they might have tried to call. I need to check my phone." Releasing her, he walked to the table. "Want me to turn yours on in case Kendra left you a message?"

"Please." That's what she'd do—call Kendra, who was probably with Quinn. Yesterday she hadn't wanted either of them to worry, but that was before a herd of buffalo had camped in the front yard. If Quinn could talk Brendan out of his foolhardy plan, great.

If not, she'd think of some other way to stop him. He was not going out there, and that was final.

19

Brendan turned on his phone and waited for the welcome screen to load. Jo didn't like his plan. Check that. She *hated* his plan.

He wasn't surprised. From her standpoint, it was almost suicidal. From his, it was the only logical move. Last night he'd been irritated by the critters' presence, but making love to Jo had put him in a more receptive frame of mind.

This morning, while he was half-asleep and fretting over the wood situation, he'd heard his Goondeen laughing. *You think you're trapped by those animals? Have you already forgotten everything I taught you?*

Almost. But when Jo had gone into the bathroom, he'd quickly put on his clothes and walked out on the porch. Quiet out there. He'd emptied his mind of negativity and filled it with kind words for these worthy beasts, descendants of those who'd nearly been hunted to extinction.

All they wanted was a little shelter from the blowing snow. By keeping the cabin warm, he was helping them. For that he needed more wood. Simple. He'd been tempted to walk to the house right then, but he couldn't let Jo wake up and find him gone. She would have freaked out.

He'd tried to come at the subject slowly this morning, hoping she'd gradually get used to the idea. She wasn't having any of it. She was scared for him and he didn't know how to calm her fears.

He had a text from Andy asking how they were doing. He texted back that they were good for now. No point in getting Andy riled up, too.

"Hi, Kendra. Listen, I don't have much battery left, so this needs to be quick. Is Quinn there? Can I talk with him?"

He turned and met Jo's determined gaze. Should have seen that coming. She was calling in the troops.

"Hi, Quinn. I'd like to put you on speaker if that's okay. I want Brendan to hear your reaction to what's going on here."

"All right." Quinn sounded carefully neutral.

Good ol' Quinn. Nothing steadier than that guy. Brendan smiled. This should be an interesting conversation. He kept his mouth shut while Jo laid out the issue as she saw it—that he was an idiot bent on his own destruction.

In the background, Kendra gasped in dismay and voiced her disapproval of his proposed course of action. He wasn't surprised by that, either. Quinn just listened.

"That's the gist of it," Jo said. "I'm hoping you can convince your brother to stay put and see if the buffalo herd leaves."

Quinn cleared his throat. "When's your wood gonna run out, bro?"

"There's no insulation in this cabin and it leaks like a sieve. If we want to keep reasonably warm, we have to keep the fire goin' full blast. I estimate we'll be out of wood by about two this afternoon."

"And even if you ration yourselves, you'll run out sometime during the night."

"Guaranteed."

"That's only if the buffalo herd sticks around," Jo said. "It might be gone in another couple of hours."

"Exactly!" Kendra said. "Why risk life and limb when you might not have a problem?"

"I seriously doubt he'll be risking life and limb." Quinn's comment brought a flurry of protests from Jo and Kendra, but he soldiered on. "I'd like to hear your assessment of these critters, little brother."

Bless Quinn Sawyer, the best brother a guy ever had. "It's all about timin'. The herd is mellow now but no tellin' if it'll stay like that. I've made contact and I'm convinced they'll give me safe passage."

"What about when you come back with the wood? I assume you'll be pulling a sled of some kind. How will they react to that?"

"I'll come walkin' in slow, keep thinkin' positive, like I always do in these situations. Should be fine."

"Then I'd say you've got this, buddy. Text us when you're back, okay?"

"*What?*" Jo had her phone in a death grip. "Did you just tell him to go ahead and let himself be gored or trampled to death?"

"Jo, he won't be." Quinn's voice gentled. "He's always had a gift for communicating with animals and he polished his skills while he was Down Under. I've seen him in action, and he—"

"These aren't like cattle, Quinn!"

"I know. Sometime when the situation's less tense and we're not talking on a phone that's about to die, I'll tell you the stories. For now, trust that he knows what he's doing. He'll be fine."

"Easy for you to say!"

"Thanks, bro." Quinn was on his side. That helped.

"Don't forget to text me later."

"I won't."

"The buffalo herd aside, are you two having fun?"

He glanced at Jo, who didn't look very happy. "We were until now. Remains to be seen if we'll continue that way."

"Good luck with that. Hey, Kendra, anything more you want to mention before we hang up?"

"Yes. Listen, Jo, I apologize. I swear I had no idea that these two are completely insane. I'll deal with this one and leave Brendan to you. That's assuming you want him and he survives his dance with the buffalo."

"I'll let you know."

"Do that. 'Bye."

"'Bye." Jo disconnected and powered down her phone.

"Look, I can tell you still don't believe I can—"

She gazed at him. "Does it matter to you that even if you pull off this stunt, I'll be worried sick the whole time?"

"Of course it does. I hate to think of you worryin'. I wish there was some way I could keep that from happenin'."

"There is. Don't go."

"I'm not willin' to take the chance that we'll be stuck here without fuel. Burnin' the furniture might not be an option, even if we decide to torch the Culbertson's stuff. The wood's likely been treated and would be unsafe to burn."

"But if you'd just wait..."

"The mood of the herd could change. I need to go now. If you want to watch from the doorway so you'll know I made it out okay, I'll wait for you to get dressed."

"I don't need to watch." She folded her arms. "Just go."

"All right." He pocketed his phone and walked to the door. Leaning against the wall, he pulled on the snow boots he'd borrowed. "I thought you respected Quinn's opinion."

"I did until he started talking nonsense. So what if you've charmed a few wild animals in your day? That's not the same as facing down an entire herd of creatures averaging two thousand pounds apiece."

"That's the point. I won't *face them down* as you say. I'll go about my business and let them go about theirs."

"Let's hope that's the way it works out." She swallowed. "Be seeing you."

"I promise you will be seein' me."

"Don't go making promises you might not be able to keep."

She was terrified for him. He crossed the room and took her in his arms. She kept hers folded in front of her, a barrier to ward off pain. "I'll keep this one, Jo. We have a lot more lovin' to do." He kissed her gently, mindful of his beard. Then he let her go.

"Damn it, Brendan!" She uncrossed her arms and grabbed him. "If you'll take off those boots, I'll make it worth your while."

"My cock is willing."

"Then listen to your cock."

"But the rest of me knows this isn't the time." He backed away. "How 'bout a raincheck?"

"I don't know. I'm pretty mad at you right now."

"I know you are. See you soon, Jo."

"You'd better."

"I will." He took his hat from a peg on the wall and opened the door.

She took a shaky breath. "You have to or you'll make a liar out of your big brother."

"I'll be back before you know it." Closing the door behind him, he stood on the porch and surveyed the herd. Most were lying down, tucked against the protected side of the house like a pack of very large sled dogs.

A few had gathered by a group of pine trees growing a slight distance from the cabin. The ginormous male stood guard halfway between the groups.

Impressive animal. Brendan greeted him with respect as his Goondeen had taught him. Then he slowly put on his hat, avoiding sudden movements, and descended the steps, his boots making deep divots in each layer of snow.

At the bottom of the steps, he looked over at the male buffalo. They were on a level plane, now, and counting the bull's hump, he was taller than Brendan's six-three. Brendan touched the brim of his hat in a brief salute and turned his back on the imposing bulk of the herd's leader.

As he trudged through knee-deep snow in the direction of the house, he listened for any indication that he was being followed. He didn't expect it, but if it happened, he'd dive for a snowdrift and hope for the best. The depth of the snow would make the bull slower, but he'd be slower, too.

The potential for disaster was always present in wild animal encounters. Jo was right about that, but his chance of survival was many times higher than she'd given him credit for. Still, he hated that he'd caused her distress. He would have avoided it if he could have.

When he was several yards away, he turned to look back. The bull had stayed put and was still watching him. What a thrill to encounter such a force of nature. He relished the challenge, always had. Jo didn't get it.

But, hey, this weekend was supposed to be about discovering whether they worked as a couple. They'd just hit their first major roadblock.

He didn't want it to be a deal-breaker, but wildlife encounters like this were highlight reels for him. If they were bad news clips for her, they had a problem.

<u>20</u>

Stupid idiot. Jo put on her boots. Wrapping her arms around her middle, she paced the area near the door. If the buffalo herd went after him, she'd hear them. She'd go out there and do what she could.

Which would be blessed little. How could he take a chance like this? He thought he was invincible, that's how. She forgave that tendency in teenagers, but a grown man should be over it.

She'd counted on Quinn to talk sense into him, but he'd been no help at all. Like Kendra had said, evidently the Sawyer brothers were insane. Kendra was already deeply committed to Quinn, but Jo hadn't....

Never mind. Better not evaluate her feelings for Brendan right now. Anger was mixed in with something else, something she wasn't ready to face.

Sure was quiet outside. He'd have had plenty of time to make his getaway. By some miracle he might have survived the first part of this stunt.

Opening the door a few inches, she checked the position of the critters. The big one, probably the buffalo that had peeked in the window and scared her to death, stood gazing down the path Brendan had taken. No sign of Brendan. She heaved a sigh of relief.

The buffalo turned his shaggy head in her direction and she quietly closed the door, heart pounding. Brendan had walked away without a problem, but that giant animal seemed to be on alert. Was he waiting his chance, poised to attack if the human returned?

Maybe she could stall that return long enough that the bull would abandon his post and join the others that were over by a grove of pine trees. They stood munching on low-hanging branches. The big guy had to be hungry, too, right?

Her battery was down to twenty percent, but that was enough to give Ida a quick call. It was the only number of theirs she'd put in her phone.

Ida sounded nervous when she answered. "Are you two okay? Is the buffalo herd still there?"

"Yes, and they—"

"Promise me you won't go out there until they're gone."

"That's why I'm calling. We're running out of wood and the electricity went off last night."

"Oh, no! Listen, we'll figure something out. Not sure what right now, but just stay put."

"That was my plan but Brendan's on his way to your house to fetch wood."

"He went outside with the buffalo there?"

"Yep, and the herd's leader looks like he's just waiting for that human to show up again. Keep Brendan there any way you can, okay? Lecture him, bribe him with pie, whatever you can think of to stall him. Maybe the herd will leave. If not, the bull might get tired of standing guard."

"How long will your wood last?"

"If I ration myself, I can make it until late this afternoon. But you won't be able to keep Brendan there that long. I know him a lot better now, and I realize how headstrong he—"

"You're newlyweds, aren't you? I thought you were from the moment I saw you two together."

"You guessed it." And guessed wrong, thank goodness. Jo had forgotten they were supposed to be married. She glanced at the crocodile ring on her finger. Should have sent it off with Brendan in case he needed the juju for his animal whisperer routine. "My phone battery's almost dead, Ida, so I'd better end the call. Please try to delay Brendan."

"We will. And I'll pray that herd decides to mosey on down the line."

"Thanks for that. 'Bye." She disconnected and turned off her phone. Now what?

The fire needed tending. She'd use as little wood as possible, but letting it go out made no sense. Since she planned to build it up a little more, might as well heat some water, take a sponge bath and put on clean clothes. And more clothes on top of that.

Folding the blanket bed in half, she made room near the fire to spread out a towel. This project would have been fun with Brendan here. Instead it was a chore to keep her from going nuts with worry.

She made short work of the job, dried off and started layering—three pairs of panties but only one bra. Layered bras would bind. She pulled on three long-sleeved tees, her skinny jeans followed by a looser pair, and her warmest sweatshirt, the one with the Guzzling Grizzly logo.

By that point she had to move away from the fire before she started sweating. With two layers of denim encasing her lower half, her walk had a zombie-like quality. Choosing a dining chair on the other side of the room, she sat down awkwardly and put on three pairs of clean socks. Good thing she'd brought extras of everything.

Her suitcase was almost empty. Nothing left except a couple of bras, a sparkly top for a nice dinner out, and two pairs of slinky pajamas that weren't designed to keep her warm but would likely get Brendan hot.

Leaving the blanket bed on the floor in the middle of the day bothered her tidy nature. Besides, the cozy dynamic had changed. She was upset with him. Scared for him. Sex was the last thing on her mind.

She shook out the bedding, rolled it up and laid it on the bare mattress. Picking up the box of condoms, she put them on the chair next to the bed.

Next she investigated the home-canned goods in the hall closet. She wasn't hungry, not with Brendan's safety hanging in the balance, but if he made it back in one piece, they'd need to eat something.

She brought several jars into the kitchen and lined them up on the counter. Looked like they'd be eating a lot of veggies, plus some peaches and plums. That was assuming the buffalo herd was still in residence when he came back. She'd hoped the weather would clear, but it was snowing harder than ever.

When she'd run out of things to do, she gave in to the urge pulling her toward the front door. Was that bull still planted in the same spot? She cracked open the door. With all her layers, the cold air didn't have as much bite.

No buffalo was standing guard at his post. Had they all left? Heart racing, she slipped out the door. Something was in her peripheral vision. She turned her head and almost passed out. The bull stood by the side of the porch, only about six feet from her.

He didn't move. Neither did she. Wasn't sure she could. His face looked like he'd dipped it in a mixing bowl of flour. Puffs of vapor from his leathery nostrils weren't that different from the ones she created with each panting breath.

His musky scent was muted, likely by the freezing weather. His matted fur could use a good brushing. *Yeah, Jo, why not offer to do that for him? He's close enough.* A bubble of hysterical laughter caught in her throat. She swallowed it.

He regarded her steadily, his deep brown eyes fringed with short, partly frozen lashes. That gaze was familiar. Eeyore, the old gray horse she shared with Mandy and stabled in Kendra's barn, often looked at her with that same world-weary expression.

With Eeyore, it was a joke. He lived a pampered life at Wild Creek Ranch. Not this guy.

His responsibilities must weigh heavily on those massive shoulders. Had to be a big job keeping the herd together, running off predators and finding food in the middle of winter.

She was still terrified of him. He could splinter the porch railing with one careless shove. He could lower that enormous head and drive a curved horn deep into her gut. But nothing in his behavior telegraphed aggression.

Then his attention shifted toward the path from the main house. A scraping sound, like something being dragged over snow, preceded the figure emerging from the swirling snow pulling a toboggan, its cargo secured with a tarp. Brendan.

He paused, as if assessing the situation. Whatever his plan had been, he wouldn't have expected her to be a part of it. Having the bull this close to the house had to be a complication. She'd added to it by coming outside.

But she dared not move. Sure as the world, fear would make her clumsy and she'd do something to startle the bull. Standing as quietly as possible seemed like the safest option. She clenched her jaw to keep her teeth from chattering.

Leaving the toboggan, Brendan started walking slowly toward the porch, hands held loosely at his sides. When he was about five yards away, he spoke in a low, soothing voice. "Makin' friends, I see."

"Uh-huh." She focused on him but kept track of the buffalo out of the corner of her eye. "You shaved."

"Ida's suggestion."

"You just left the toboggan."

"For now. They won't mess with it. Just a load of seasoned wood. Critical for us, worthless to them."

"I worry about you coming any closer."

"No worries. I'm goin' to stroll up there, cool as a cucumber, and escort you inside. Don't move until I get there."

She began to shake. "W-what if he goes after you?"

"He won't if we don't make any sudden moves. Take slow, easy breaths. Try to relax."

Oh, sure. Relax. She'd do her best. She concentrated on drawing air gently into her lungs. Very cold air that tickled her throat. Made her want to cough. *Don't!*

He started up the steps and the bull snorted. She almost peed her pants.

"Your eyes are like saucers."

"How romantic."

"That part comes later."

"Assuming we live."

"We will." He stood inches away, his chest heaving, his gaze intense. Clearly he wasn't all that relaxed, either. He reached around her and gradually pushed the door open. "Step backward, but carefully. Don't rush it."

"Grab my arm, please. My legs are wobbly."

His firm grip was the best thing that had happened to her since he'd left the cabin. She almost lost control and threw herself into his arms.

"Easy does it, Jo."

"Right." If he hadn't steadied her, she likely would have stumbled and crashed into the door. That wouldn't have gone well. Instead she slipped through as noiselessly as she'd come out earlier.

Still holding her arm, Brendan followed. He closed the door with a soft click. "Dear God." He knocked his hat to the floor as he jerked her hard against him and claimed her mouth with bold intent.

She clutched the back of his head and matched the urgent thrust of his tongue with one of her own. He groaned and changed the angle, taking the kiss deeper as he unbuttoned his jacket. "Need you," he murmured against her mouth.

"Need you, too." She shoved the jacket off his shoulders.

He let her go long enough to lay it on the table. "Where are the—okay, see 'em." He cupped her ass, hoisted her up and carried her to the bed. "Why do you feel so padded?"

"I put on a bunch of clothes to save on wood."

"That's resourceful." He set her down and reached for the hem of her sweatshirt.

"Thanks." She nudged off her boots and lifted her arms so he could tug off the sweatshirt.

He tossed it aside and eyed her shirt. "How many of those?"

"Three."

He started to laugh. "No wonder you looked more substantial than when I left. Let's do this in one go." He pulled off all three together and glanced at her. "I only see one bra."

"That's all."

"Bonus." Kneeling in front of her, he reached behind her back and unhooked the clasp. "I figured you'd be dressed when I got back. When I was pullin' that toboggan, I pictured undressin' you again. That kept me goin'."

"Bet you didn't picture me all layered up."

"I didn't, but I accept the challenge." He slid her bra off and placed a light kiss on each of her nipples. "You smell great."

"Sponge bath."

"Without me?"

"I—"

"Never mind." He unfastened the waistband of her jeans. "Double jeans?"

"And three pairs of panties."

"Crickey, woman! You're like a video game where the tasks keep gettin' harder. But I'm also gettin' harder, so I'm motivated."

"I never imagined you'd be the one who had to take off all the—"

"Didn't you?" He unzipped both pairs of jeans and hooked his thumbs in the elastic of her panties. "Why not?"

"It seemed like things had…changed."

He paused and met her gaze. "We had a little hiccup. Doesn't have to become a big thing unless you want it to."

She took a shaky breath. "I don't know what I want."

"That's fair." He gave her a lopsided grin. "But after gettin' this far, seems a shame to put all those layers back on."

"You'd stop?"

"Yea, yea, I would. Not my preferred course of action, but if you—"

"Please don't stop."

"Alrighty, then." With one swift tug, he divested her of jeans, panties, and even socks. "Let's have us some fun."

21

Sex couldn't solve every problem in a relationship, but Brendan gave it credit for reducing the size of the issues to something manageable. Besides, making love to Jo was a joy and a privilege. He didn't want to miss an opportunity to indulge.

Having a continuous fire for nearly twelve hours had warmed the interior of the cabin enough that they could roll around on the mattress nudie and not freeze their privates. And roll around they did. He delayed suiting up so they could play a little bit in the pale light of day.

He explored the terrain of her responsive body for a while, kissing and licking his way along all her secret places until he managed to make her come. After that she demanded equal time. She would have given him a climax, too, but he pulled away before she could accomplish that.

He reached for the box sitting on the chair. "I want to be inside you." He opened a foil package and rolled on the condom. "I want to feel your climax squeezin' my cock." He guided her onto her back and moved between her thighs. "I want to watch your eyes shimmer with happiness after you come."

"They shimmer?"

"Oh, yea, they do." He propped himself on his forearms and slid easily into her hot channel. "And because we have more light, I'll be able to see better. I love lookin' at you, Jo."

She cupped his face in both hands. "I love looking at you, too." She smoothed her fingertips over his eyebrows. "You have great brows."

"Oh?" He waggled them. "How so?"

"Expressive. And the salt and pepper effect makes you seem really wise."

"Which I am. Wise enough to be right here with you, my cock buried to the hilt."

She twined her legs around his, locking him in even tighter. "I like the way we fit."

"Couldn't get any better." He eased back and rocked forward. "It's like we were made for each other."

She gazed up at him. "Do you believe in that?"

"I think so." More every hour.

"Not me."

He settled in a bit deeper. "I may regret askin', but have you had better?"

"No." She pressed her fingers into his glutes.

"As good, then?"

"No."

"Me, either." He began to move, each stroke bringing more certainty. She was right for him. But was he right for her? Only she would know.

Clearly she enjoyed making love with him. He'd learned when to slow down, when to speed up, how to make a subtle shift in position that made her gasp in delight. As her climax drew near, her skin took on a rosy glow. He hadn't been able to see that during the night.

So lovely. His chest grew tight with longing. He wanted her—in his arms, in his life. But there were no guarantees.

He chose the pace that would make her come and she did, pressing her fingers into his ass, arching her back, crying out his name. He gave himself the gift of climaxing right after her, sharing the heat and joy, murmuring her name. *Jo. My beautiful Jo.*

As their breathing slowed, cool air tickled his bare back. The fire had died down and the cabin was chilly again. He reached for the roll of blankets, grabbed one edge and managed to cover them up, sort of.

Propped on his forearms, he gazed down at her post-climax face. "There's that happiness shimmer."

"How could I not be? You make me feel so good."

"Ditto."

She touched his cheek. "Who loaned you a razor?"

"Andy, after Ida told him to. She was determined I would shave before I came back here. Since I knew I'd want to kiss the daylights out of you the minute I walked in the door, I went along with it. Kinda funny how she insisted, though. Then she wanted me to take a shower since we didn't have hot water, but that seemed unfair to you."

"She was pushing those things because I called and asked her to delay you as best she could."

"Why?"

"After you left, I peeked out the door and saw the bull stationed out front, like he was guarding the area. I figured if you stayed away longer, he might give up his post."

"Instead he moved closer to the house."

"I didn't know that. I thought he was gone, and I came out to make sure, but—"

"I lost ten years of my life when I saw you standing on the porch."

"I made things tougher for you. Didn't mean to."

"It worked out." He traced his finger around her full mouth. "But if anything had happened to you..."

"Now you know how I felt when you walked out that door."

"But I—" He abandoned what he'd been about to say. She'd tensed, as if preparing for an argument. He didn't want one. "Anyway, now it makes sense that Ida kept temptin' me with apple pie."

"You didn't eat any?"

"I politely refused. Several times."

"You love that pie!"

"Not as much as I...um, wanted to get back to you." Whoa. A significant statement had almost leaped right out of his mouth. He hadn't seen it coming. Those statements were supposed to be delivered after much inner debate. He'd skipped that step.

"If you didn't eat anything while you were there, you must be starving."

"Not anymore."

"For food."

"Oh, that." He grinned. "I could eat."

"I hauled out some of the canned fruit and veggies. We could have a veggie stew and canned fruit for dessert."

"That works." He eased away from her. "After I take my walk down the hall, I can bring your coat or your clothes, whichever you want."

"My coat, please."

He winked at her. "Great choice. It's mine, too, but I might have to get dressed once we need that wood I left outside."

"But you'll wait as long as possible, right? In case they leave?"

"I will." The panic in her voice told him she thought he'd just been lucky. She didn't believe he had the skills to avoid a confrontation with that bull. No point in debating it. Yet.

When he returned from the bathroom, she was already up, wearing her coat and tending the fire. She'd retrieved his coat from the floor and laid it on the bed.

He shoved his arms in the sleeves and buttoned it as he went over to the fireplace. "You can add more wood than that. I brought plenty."

"But it's outside. We can make do with a smaller fire."

He didn't want to make do with a smaller fire. He'd gone after the wood because they were snowbound in a cabin with no other source of heat. He liked being warm.

But his trip for wood was a sore point with Jo. He'd bide his time and make do with a smaller fire.

She glanced over her shoulder. "Your silence speaks volumes."

"Which one of those books are you readin'?"

"The one titled *I Brought the Damn Wood So Let Me Go Get It, Already.*"

He laughed. "I'm particularly fond of that story."

"I know you are." She hung the tongs in the cast iron holder and replaced the screen. "I'm not. I prefer the one titled *Going Outside Makes Jo Nervous So I Won't.*"

"You'll be surprised to know that's the one I was readin'. That's why I kept my mouth shut about the puny fire."

"You say puny. I say adequate."

"Are you plannin' to heat up those veggies?"

"Yes."

"Could take a while."

"Then we can have some fruit while the veggies are warming."

"That's fine." He reached into his pocket. "And you can be chargin' your phone while we eat."

"A portable charger?" Her face lit up. "Did you borrow that from the Culbertsons?"

"I did. Should have thought to bring mine on this trip. Usually do, but—"

"So do I. I remember thinking we'd be at a luxury resort so I wouldn't need it. Wow, this is great. I'll get my phone. You need to text Quinn to let him know you're alive."

"I will right now." He took his phone out of his other pocket and sent a quick text to his brother. "Does this make my trip to the main house sit any better with you?"

"No, afraid not." She brought over her phone and power cord. "I like having a working phone, and thanks for bringing this, but it wasn't worth risking your life."

"I wasn't riskin'—"

"Don't keep saying that!" Her eyes snapped with fury. "Just because you think you weren't in danger doesn't make it true."

"You're shakin'." The depth of her anger astonished him.

"Because I'm still really mad at you for disregarding your own safety. Damn, I can't even plug in my—"

"Let me." He pocketed his phone, took everything from her quivering hands and walked over to the table.

"I'll assemble our stew." She stomped into the kitchen, although wearing only socks meant she didn't achieve a decent stomp.

"Stay away from sharp objects."

"Ha, ha."

He plugged in her phone and his. Quinn had texted back a thumbs-up icon. A long talk with him would be nice right now. His big brother had always been better at untangling situations like this. A private confab wasn't a viable option, so he'd have to figure it out on his own.

Okay. What if she'd come to care for him as much as he cared for her? What if his leaving for the main house had filled her with the same stark terror that had gripped him when he'd arrived to find her less than six feet from that massive bull?

She'd said as much earlier. *Now you know how I felt.* She cared enough to not want him dead.

That was the good news. The bad news? She didn't respect his abilities or his judgment. That was a problem.

22

The veggie stew Jo put together took forever to heat up because of the smaller fire she'd insisted on. She and Brendan polished off a jar of peaches long before the stew was ready. But she was determined to make the wood last until the buffalo herd wandered off.

Brendan clearly didn't agree with her strategy, but he'd left management of the wood supply to her for now. He'd also put on his clothes. She had, too, just not as many layers as before.

She alternately watched the stew, babied the fire and peered out the window near the bed. It afforded her a view of the grove of trees and those critters were still gathered there, darn it.

She glanced at Brendan, who sat at the table checking weather and road conditions on his phone. An occasional ping told her he was sending and receiving texts, too. "Why don't they just leave?"

He looked up. "Maybe they heard that another storm's comin' in on the heels of this one."

"You're kidding."

"Not kiddin'. The emergency road crews and the utility folks are goin' nuts."

"Is everything okay at Wild Creek Ranch?"

"Everyone's fine."

"That's good." Then he had been exchanging texts with Quinn. She'd considered doing the same with Kendra, but what could she truthfully say that wouldn't be alarming?

She took a calming breath. "I didn't ask you about your truck. I don't suppose Seth can work on it until the weather clears."

"The power outage is the real problem. He has a shed where he could do the work but he can't run the space heater when they're operatin' with only a generator."

"Are they doing okay up at the house?"

"Andy says they're fine but he's worried about us. He'd love to get a helicopter to airlift us out."

"That seems a bit extreme."

"I told him that. I have this handled." There was a trace of defiance in his voice, as if he dared her to say otherwise.

She chose not to.

He went back to looking at his phone. "I seriously doubt Andy could get us a helicopter, anyway. The weather's a deterrent and emergency crews are stretched thin."

"I'm sure. If Andy and Seth hadn't come along, we could be in even worse shape."

"I'd have figured out somethin'."

"I know, but I'm just saying—"

"I would have protected you, Jo. Whatever it took."

"That last part is what worries me."

"What do you—"

"Never mind." She headed back to the kitchen, picked up a long-handled spoon and went over to stir the veggies. At last they were steaming and a few bubbles popped up. "Looks like the stew's ready."

"I'll help." He left his phone on the table and grabbed an oven mitt before lifting the kettle from the fire and carrying it to the kitchen.

"Just warning you that it'll be a little bland. I found salt and pepper, but that's it."

"No worries." He set the kettle on the stove. "Ida wanted to give me containers of food, but I couldn't take the chance. Those animals have to be hungry."

"They're herbivores, right?" Jo handed him a bowl and the long-handled spoon. "Take as much as you—"

"Ah, no." He waved her off. "Ladies first."

"All right." She dished herself a generous amount and carried the bowl over to the fire.

"Take the easy chair."

"Okay. Thanks." Despite the tension between them, he was unfailingly polite. She gave him points for that.

He came over with his bowl and sat in the dining chair next to her. "To answer your question, yes, they're herbivores, but there might've been something to attract them in those containers she wanted to send with me."

"I agree. Not worth the risk. But then neither was—"

"Hey."

She looked over at him.

Irritation flickered in his gray eyes. Irritation directed at her. He took a deep breath. "Could we agree to talk about something else?"

"Yes."

"Good."

But what? Quinn and Brendan might agree the situation was under control, but she didn't think so. And she had no clue what to do about it.

She ate in silence as the fire flickered weakly on the grate. If she didn't put on another log, it would be reduced to embers soon. The cabin was decidedly colder than it had been an hour ago.

She put her half-finished bowl of stew on the floor and stood. "We could use another log."

"Only three left."

"I know." She chose the smallest of the three and laid it carefully over the remnants of the other two that were nearly gone. The new log caught at once and flared up, providing a comforting crackle and pop. "That's better."

"If you say so."

So he was irritated, was he? Might as well lob out the question that had bugged her ever since meeting him. She picked up her bowl of stew. "Why haven't you ever married?"

He stared at her. "You want to talk about that *now*?"

"It's a different subject."

"Yea, yea, but—"

"At the beginning of our trip you said I deserved a decent answer. Are you ready to give me one?"

He cleared his throat. "Guess so."

"Have you even been engaged to anyone?"

"No, ma'am."

"That's pretty unusual, don't you think?"

"So I've been told." He scraped the bottom of his bowl and took his last bite.

"I can't believe Australia doesn't have some wonderful women living there."

"Plenty of 'em."

"Was that the problem? You had too much fun playing the field? Didn't want to limit yourself to—"

"Are you goin' to let me answer or just keep firin' questions?" His gaze was hot, but with anger this time, not passion.

"Go ahead."

He set his bowl on the floor and took a deep breath. "Yea, I enjoyed havin' fun with different women." He looked at the fire instead of at her. "Each one was special in her own way."

That hit a nerve. But she'd asked for it. If she didn't want to hear about his romantic history, she shouldn't have asked.

"Several times I wondered if this was the one, if I wanted to spend the rest of my life with her." He stretched his legs toward the meager fire. "I'd spend time debatin' it and the answer was always the same. I couldn't picture a lifetime with that person."

"You never found the right woman." What a depressingly common excuse. None of them were good enough. Blech.

"Oh, I very well might have found her. Many times over. But I wasn't the right man. I wasn't ready for marriage."

She blinked. He was taking the responsibility because he was lacking? Refreshing attitude.

"Some people are ready for that step early. Quinn was like that. Good partner material from the get-go."

"That's great news for Kendra."

"He'll make her very happy, but then she's cut from the same cloth. They're perfect for each other. Gives me hope that such a thing is possible."

"I know what you mean." The fire was dying again. She resisted adding another log so soon. "It's good to know love like that exists."

"I've taken it one step further. Watching Kendra and Quinn together gives me hope that such a thing is possible for me, personally."

"Oh." Her chest tightened.

"I'm a classic example of a late bloomer. Working with my Goondeen matured me. I had a couple of long talks with Quinn when I was here over Christmas. I think I'm finally ready to sign on for the long haul."

Her stomach hollowed out. "If you can find the right woman."

"Yea, yea." He sighed. "Thought I had." He stood without looking at her. "I'm goin' out to get the wood."

She jumped up. "*Please* don't. They could leave any minute!"

He faced her, his expression resolute. "You're right, they could. But we're down to the nubs and this cabin is losin' heat fast. Another storm is comin' in. I want that wood inside now."

"What if you get hurt out there? What happens then?"

"I won't."

"You don't know that!"

"Yea, I do. I believe in my abilities, Jo. Unfortunately, you don't."

"Wait." She grabbed his arm. Solid. Strong. But no match for a two-thousand-pound wild creature that might take a notion to kill him. "Here's an idea. I should have thought of it before. You say you can communicate with those animals, right?"

"In a manner of speakin'. But you don't believe that I—"

"Doesn't matter what I believe. You **do**, and this is at least worth a try. Communicate to them that they need to leave. Would that work?"

"No."

"Why not?"

"Because I'm not doin' it. They have two calves with them and I—"

"Two? I thought only one."

"On my way out I saw two and one didn't look healthy. This cabin, which is givin' off heat, and the grove of trees, which provides some food, is givin' the herd a restin' place. It might save the life of that calf. I don't know if they'd leave if I asked them, but I won't. They need to make that decision for themselves. 'Scuse me." He gently removed her hand and walked over to the door.

His boots sat there, waiting. His hat hung on a peg nearby. He must have placed his boots and hat in readiness for this moment.

"What about *your* life? Isn't that worth anything?"

He leaned against the wall and tugged on his boots. "It's extremely precious to me. That's why I'm spendin' every second of it doin' what I think is right."

Whatever it takes? Her heart thundered, making her ears buzz. "I'm so afraid for you."

"I know." His expression softened. "Wish you weren't." He settled his hat on his head. "I'll need your help. This'll take a couple of trips, and I'll be loaded down each time I get to the door. If you could listen for me and open it, I'd—"

"Oh, I'll be listening for you, all right." Steel bands of anxiety tightened around her chest. "You can count on it."

"Then I'll see you in a bit." He touched two fingers to the brim of his hat and opened the door.

She lowered her voice. "Is he still by the porch?"

"Yea, yea." His tone was light, conversational. "Brought some friends. And that peaked-lookin' calf." He closed the door.

She held her breath. He was still talking, but not to her. He was carrying on a soft conversation with the buffalo.

23

A total of six animals, five adults and one sickly calf, had gathered beside the porch. The adults had the calf surrounded. Brendan kept his arms at his sides and avoided direct eye contact as he asked after the health of the calf.

Despite the imposing bulk of these critters, technically they were classified as prey, not predators. He was the predator in this equation. With five of them gathered, they were fragrant, and some of that could be the result of fear. Convincing them he wasn't a threat wasn't easy, but he'd done it twice before. The calf hadn't been in the mix, though.

"Here's the deal, guys and gals." He kept his tone conversational. "It's cozy here by the cabin 'cause the place leaks like a canteen swatted by a porcupine's tail. Cold air flows in. If we keep a fire goin', warm air flows out. We're runnin' out of wood, though."

The bull snorted and changed position, putting himself on the outside of the group and facing Brendan. He stood ready to guard and protect. And attack, if necessary.

Brendan's pulse rate climbed. He took several slow breaths to calm himself. "I get that you're worried, mate. I'm askin' you to let me pass so I can fetch the wood that's sittin' on that toboggan over there." He resisted the urge to point it out. The less movement, the better. "I'll do my best not to disturb anyone."

He waited, still not making eye contact but aware of the bull's every twitch or shifting of weight. The big guy held his ground but didn't advance toward the path Brendan would have to take to reach the toboggan.

Now or never. He edged toward the steps and started down. His previous divots had filled in some, but he used them to help muffle the crunch of his boots digging into the snow.

He kept track of the bull from the corner of his eye, but once he was off the porch, he had to turn his back on the animal. Tuning in to any sounds coming from behind, he made his way toward the toboggan.

A layer of snow covered the canvas tarp. He brushed the snow away gradually. Then he untied the tarp, folded it and tucked it under the toboggan. A blowing tarp could stampede cattle, so odds were good it would do the same with these critters.

Andy and Seth had helped him tie the wood into ten bundles with rope handles for ease of carrying. If he could manage five each time, he'd get everything in two trips.

Moments later he started back with two bundles dangling in each hand and one on his back. He'd used his belt like a bandolier to secure the fifth bundle. The male buffalo blew steam from his nostrils and watched his slow approach.

If the bull charged...Brendan quickly wiped the image from his mind and replaced it with one of the buffalo standing quietly and allowing him to pass unchallenged. He visualized walking calmly up the steps, across the porch and through the cabin door with his load of wood.

As he walked he sent messages of friendship to each of the animals huddled near the cabin and a salute of respect to the bull. Almost there. Close enough to catch the musky scent. *Stand quietly, mate. I'm a friend. I wish you well.*

Breathing slowly, he mounted the steps. Behind him, the bull snorted again. *Just lettin' me know you're there. That's okay, mate. Thanks for lettin' me pass.*

He crossed the porch and the door swung open. He stepped inside, tracking snow. "Close it real slow."

The door clicked shut as he lowered the bundles. "Thanks."

"Is that it?" Jo came to stand in front of him, her eyes wide and her breathing fast. "Are you done?"

"One more load like this. There were ten." He unbuckled his belt and eased the wood from his back.

"We don't need any more. This is plenty."

"I'm going back for the rest."

"Brendan, damn it! You got this much. Why push your luck?"

His jaw clenched. She still didn't understand. "It's not luck." He rolled up his belt and shoved it in his pocket. "See you in a bit."

She groaned. "I can't believe this."

"Exactly." He opened the door with more force than he'd intended, startling the critters by the porch and upsetting the delicate balance he'd achieved earlier. Hell. Anger was a stupid luxury he couldn't afford. The bull tensed. Brendan did, too.

Behind him, Jo drew in a sharp breath. Then she quietly closed the door.

Relax. Easy does it. Get your mojo back. Slow, even breaths.

The bull lowered his head and pawed a groove in the snow. Clearly not happy.

Brendan let air seep from his lungs in a steady release of tension. "We're still okay, mate." He talked to the bull as if they were sharing a pint at the pub. "Just havin' a disagreement with the lady in my life. You know how that goes."

The pawing stopped and the massive head swung in his direction.

"Yea, yea, bet you know what I'm talkin' 'bout. Didn't mean to upset you, though." Once again he avoided looking straight at the bull. "Bad enough she and I are crossways without carryin' it over to my relationship with you."

The change in the animal was subtle. A slight lowering of the eyelids, a slackening of the jaw.

Brendan took a step across the porch, and another. "I need those last five bundles of wood, mate, so I'd appreciate your cooperation. Once I haul that in, I won't need to disturb you again for quite a while. The cabin will be warmer, too. Benefits us all." He started down the steps.

So far, so good. Turning his back on the bull took more guts this time. He recited the mantra his Goondeen had taught him—*respect and friendship*—as he slowly pivoted toward the toboggan.

He'd made it halfway when the crunch of snow behind him indicated he was not making the journey alone. A musky odor told him who was following him. "Coming along to see what this is all about, are you?" *Respect and friendship, respect and friendship.*

He paused beside the toboggan. Securing the fifth bundle to his back became a whole lot less important. He'd go back with four and call it good. Assuming he'd be allowed to go back at all.

He picked up two bundles in each hand with the attention he'd give to sizzling sticks of dynamite. Then he faced the bull, who stood about ten feet away, blocking his path.

"Lead the way, mate. I'll bring up the rear." It was a ridiculous thing to say. But he placed the image firmly in his mind, anyway.

And the bull *did it*, swiveling toward the house and walking slowly in that direction. Brendan waited until the animal had almost returned to his original position before following.

He couldn't wait to tell Quinn about this. But before he could spread that story around, he had to make it onto the porch and through the door. That wasn't a slam-dunk, especially when the buffalo stopped right next to the steps.

Then the animal looked back at him.

"I can't go up on the porch unless you move, my friend."

The bull looked away and remained planted in front of the steps.

"Do you want me to ask permission? No worries. I humbly ask your permission to go back inside the—" Then it hit him. Should've figured it out long ago. "This is your special place, isn't it?"

The animal still didn't budge.

"No wonder you peered in the window last night. You arrived in your special place to find intruders. Andy told me buffalo used to migrate through here. It wasn't just some random herd, was it? It was you guys."

Once again, the bull turned his head in Brendan's direction.

"Thank you for lettin' us share your space, mate. At least we've provided some benefit by makin' the area around the cabin warmer, but still, we did barge in uninvited. I apologize. If you'll be kind enough to let me pass, I'll head inside and stoke up the fire. Warmth for all."

The wood was getting heavier by the second, but he stood quietly, respectfully, waiting for the answer. All things considered, the buffalo herd had behaved with remarkable restraint.

At last the bull ambled over to join the small group beside the porch. Possibly more grout was missing there and they enjoyed the additional heat. Or maybe they'd always preferred the cozy area beside the porch and had been afraid to claim it with humans lurking inside.

"Thank you very much." He mounted the steps. "I'll make sure we mind our manners from now on. And I'll speak to Andy and Seth, too. Tryin' to run you off with their pickup a couple of years ago wasn't cool. Probably why you didn't come back for a while."

He gave them one last glance before he crossed the porch. They didn't like having him there. They merely tolerated his presence. Consequently, he wouldn't bug them again unless he absolutely had to. That meant being closed in the cabin with Jo.

He couldn't predict how that would go. Another storm was coming, so they weren't likely to get out of there in the next twenty-four hours. They weren't happy with one another, but he still wanted her and he'd bet his entire life savings that she still wanted him.

As he walked across the porch, the cabin door swung open and he stepped inside.

She closed it behind him. "Four? I thought you were determined to get—"

"Left one. It was the prudent thing to do."

"Prudent? You?"

He put down the wood and turned to her. Swallowing his initial snarky response, he met her gaze. "I've terrified you, haven't I, Jo?"

Her disapproving glare gradually dissolved and her chin trembled. Tears swam in her eyes and she blinked rapidly. Her voice was a mere whisper. "Yes."

"I'm sorry."

"M-me, too."

He took a step closer.

She took a step back. "I think…I think it's best if we don't…"

"Hug?" Oh, boy. This was gonna hurt.

"Or…anything."

He swallowed. "We're liable to be stuck here for another twenty-four hours, maybe more."

"I understand." She took a shaky breath. "But having sex when we both know this isn't going to work…"

"Are you positive 'bout that?"

"Yes. So are you."

"Yea, yea, I have my doubts, but that doesn't mean we're dead in the water."

"I think it does. We've had fun in bed, but when the chips are down…we aren't in sync at all."

"I can't argue with that, but I was hopin' that we—"

"Could still have a good time while we're stranded here?"

"When you say it like that, it sounds like you think all I care about is sex. That's not the case. What we have goes beyond enjoyin' good climaxes."

"That's what makes this so tough." She took another quivering breath. "But I can't let that blind me to our differences. If I keep having sex with you, it might." She crossed her arms. "So we're done."

The finality in her voice sucker-punched him in the gut. He couldn't speak, so he just nodded, picked up the wood and carried it over to the wood bin.

24

The ban on sexy times had seemed doable while Jo was caught up in the drama of Brendan's daredevil behavior. She'd been scared to death and furious with him for making her go through such an ordeal.

But now the danger was past and the argument was over. He'd made tea and poured them each a mug. Then he'd chosen to sit in the dining chair by the fire while he kept up with the weather news on his phone and texted.

He'd left the easy chair empty, quite likely on purpose, in case she wanted to join him. She didn't dare get that close.

The roaring fire he'd created allowed him to ditch his coat. Wearing only a denim shirt with the top couple of buttons undone and snug jeans, he was way too approachable. Even looking at his sock feet turned her on. The term *cabin fever* took on a whole new meaning.

She retreated with her phone to the table, where she needed her sweatshirt to keep warm, but that was okay. The more layers, the better. Now that the immediate crisis was over, she could update Kendra.

Or more accurately, give Kendra her side of the story. Brendan was probably texting his side to Quinn. And since Quinn and Kendra shared everything…yeah, time to give Kendra a more balanced picture.

She brought up Kendra's contact info and began typing. *Don't know what you've heard, but Brendan hauled in the extra wood without getting himself killed.*

Kendra texted back immediately. *I heard. Also heard that you're unhappy with him.*

That's putting it mildly. Her adrenaline level spiked. Texting Kendra was a good idea. It would keep her focused on the issue. *He took a terrible risk. Then he wasn't satisfied with bringing in five bundles of wood. He had to go back for the rest. He thinks he's a buffalo whisperer.*

Quinn does say that he has a gift for communicating with animals.

Yeah, well, these animals are HUGE. Have you ever seen one up close?

No. Just from a distance.

He could so easily have been killed. Honestly, it was like a stunt one of our kids might've pulled when they were teenagers.

So what's your status, now? How does it stand between you two?

Quinn didn't say?

He just said it didn't sound good.

I've told him no more sex.

Seriously? What else is there to do in a one-room cabin?

Drink tea. Avoid each other. Check the weather report. Text you guys.

I wish we could talk about this. Can you call me?

Not now. He's right across the room.

So you can't get away from each other at all?

Not really.

How's that working out?

Not well.

Frustrated much?

Yeah.

I'm sorry, sweetie. What if you called a truce just until you get out of there? Would that be so bad?

Yep, sure would. Time to switch topics. *How's Mandy doing?*

Great. She would text you, except she wants to leave you alone to enjoy your weekend. I haven't told her the whole story.

Thanks for that. I can fill her in later, once I'm back.

I wish you could call me.

I will if I can. Brendan's on the move. TTYL. She exited the screen.

He brought his phone over and laid it on the table. "I'm goin' to try that sponge bath routine."

"Out here?" Her voice squeaked. Embarrassing.

He gave her a teasing glance. "Would that bother you?"

"Um, no, no. I can just—"

"Liar. And while we're on the subject, why are you sittin' way over here instead of in a cozy easy chair by the fire?"

"I'm fine over here."

He gazed at her. "If sittin' next to me is too temptin', I'll switch with you."

"That's not necessary. Enjoy the easy chair."

"I just might, after my sponge bath. By the way, what's your plan for tonight?"

"Meaning?"

"We'll both need to stay by the fire. I'll keep it going, but we'll have to share the blankets."

"If you keep to your side, I'll keep to mine."

"Yea, yea, I'm sure that'll work."

"When I make up my mind about something, I stick to it."

"I do believe that. But just so you know, I won't think less of you if you decide to change your mind."

"I won't."

"Alrighty, then. I'll go fetch some water in the kettle and warm it up for my sponge bath."

"Go right ahead." What the hell was she supposed to do if he stripped down? Her panties were already damp from the prospect.

While he filled the cast iron kettle at the sink, she got up and walked around the bed to peer out the window. Maybe the herd of buffalo had left. Nope. But was it her imagination, or had the snow let up?

She turned around. "When was the last time..." She lost her place in the sentence as he leaned over to hang the kettle above the fire. The soft denim of his jeans cupped his firm ass so perfectly...

He straightened and faced her. "When I did what?"

"Um..." What had she started to ask him? Oh, yeah. The weather. "The snow seems to be letting up. Have you seen anything different on the weather report?"

"Not last time I looked." He glanced at the snow falling outside the window. "I see what you mean. Let me check." He walked over to the table, picked up his phone and tapped on the screen. "Huh."

"What?"

"The second blizzard that was supposed to hit has veered northward. This part of the state won't get it, after all. Good news. I need to text Andy in case he hasn't seen this." He quickly tapped out a message.

"It's excellent news. What time is it?"

Even though he was holding his phone, he looked at the watch on his wrist. "Four-thirty. Why?"

"Just wondered how long before it starts getting dark. Not a whole lot of daylight left."

"Why does that matter?"

"If the buffalo herd moves, they'll probably leave during the night."

"Makes sense. They arrived during the night." He held her gaze. "You think the change in weather could mean they'll head on down the road?"

"Maybe."

"That's only part of the puzzle, though. We need the roads to be cleared and my truck to be operational."

"True."

"Any way you look at it, we're not gettin' out of here tonight."

"No." She avoided looking at the bed. She'd boasted that she could stick with a decision once she'd made it. This one would require all her resources.

"Since that's the case, and it's Saturday night, I'm goin' to take my bath, whether I need it or not." Putting down his phone, he walked over to the fireplace, put on his gloves and took the steaming kettle off its hook. "I'll be in the bathroom if you need me for anythin'."

"You're not going to do it out here by the fire?"

"Considered it. Decided that would just be mean, you bein' on a short fuse and all."

"Who said I was?"

"Nobody. I can see it in your eyes." He carried the steaming kettle down the hall toward the bathroom.

"It'll be dark in there."

"I'll use the light on my phone." He went inside and closed the door.

Blowing out a breath, she picked up her phone.

Kendra answered right away. "Hey, there! Did he go back outside to commune with the buffalo?"

"He's in the bathroom taking a sponge bath. He said he didn't want to do it out here because I have a short fuse. Did you tell—"

"Of course not. I don't tell Quinn *everything*. But listen, while we have this golden opportunity, let me say that Quinn's been giving me the deets on his brother, and Brendan might not have been taking the huge risk you thought he was."

"That's what you think. He might be fine with one wild animal, but he could have ended up getting run down by twenty or thirty of them. The two guys who live on this property are scared spit-less of these critters. They—"

"But you needed the wood, right?"

"We did, but if we'd started rationing earlier, we...whose side are you on, anyway?"

"Yours, Jo. Always yours. But what if Brendan's got Tarzan-like abilities? What if he's a true-blue hero, a combo of Crocodile Dundee and Tarzan? If you could hear Quinn's stories, you—"

"You're describing a fantasy, Kendra. This is a flesh-and-blood man who could have died today if he hadn't been so damn lucky. I can't get involved with someone that reckless."

"Did he tell you about his spiritual teacher over in Australia?"

"Yes." She glanced down at the crocodile ring. "I'm wearing the ring that guy gave him."

"He gave it to you?"

"He loaned it to me because we had to pretend—"

"Oh, right, right. Brendan told Quinn about the fake marriage thing. Quinn said the old Brendan would have freaked out at the idea. The new Brendan thought it was cool."

"I can't say the same. I was a little freaked out."

"Flashbacks to Robert?"

"Yep. And before you say it, I know I have issues with trusting a man's judgment. I'm willing to work on that, but not when I'm dealing with a delusional guy who thinks the laws of nature don't apply to him. Brendan's judgment is totally whacked."

"I get why you think so."

"Thanks."

"But, and I offer this lovingly, as your best friend in the whole world—you could be wrong."

"I could be, but I'm not. I'm—" A cry of pain from the bathroom was followed by a stream of pithy swear words. "Gotta go. Sounds like Crocodile Dundee just did something to himself. I'll text later." She disconnected, put down her phone and started toward the bathroom. "What's the matter?"

"It's damned cramped in here, that's what's the matter! I leaned over to wash my donger and smacked my head on the damned vanity. It's bleedin' like a sonofabitch. Blood's gettin' everywhere, but I can't see worth shit, so I don't—"

"I'm coming in."

"Let me grab a towel."

"Don't worry about that. Just move back so I don't hit you with the door."

"I have to worry about it. If you get a look at my donger you'll lose your resolve and it'll be all my fault."

"Then I won't look at it." She opened the door. "Come out in the hall so I can see what you did to your head."

"Yea, yea, okay." Clutching one towel around his hips and holding a second blood-stained one to his head, he stepped out of the bathroom. "It doesn't hurt much but it's messy as hell."

"Would you tell me if it hurt a lot?"

"Um, likely not. But this really doesn't."

A wave of tenderness caught her by surprise. He was in this fix because he'd taken her feelings into account. How ironic that he'd come out of the buffalo incident unscathed and was bleeding after trying to wash up in the bathroom.

She took a breath. "Let's go out by the fire where the light's better. I have some Band-Aids and ointment in my suitcase. You can finish your sponge bath out there." She turned to lead the way down the hall.

"I hope you understand how that's likely to turn out."

She glanced over her shoulder. He hadn't moved. "I have a pretty good idea. We'll call it a temporary truce."

A warm light filled his gaze. "Okay." His voice was as warm as his gaze. "And by the way, I didn't hit my head on purpose. But if I'd known it would change things, even temporarily, I would have."

She laughed. The charming rogue was back. She could deal with that side of Brendan Sawyer.

25

Brendan had been attempting to follow Quinn's advice by washing up in the bathroom. As he and Quinn had exchanged texts this afternoon, his big brother had recommended polite accommodation regarding Jo's moratorium on sex.

He was grateful for the suggestion. Initially he'd planned to take his sponge bath in the living room in front of the fire and let her deal with it. The bathroom was a difficult venue—cold, dark and tiny.

Making the heroic sacrifice to go in there had paid unexpected dividends. He shouldn't have shut the door and plunged himself into total darkness, but creating an extra barrier had added a touch of super-accommodation that he hadn't been able to resist.

Damned if it hadn't turned out great. Holding a bloody hand towel to his head while keeping a bath towel secured around his hips, he was no help whatsoever with setting up in the living room. He wasn't crazy about being waited on, but clearly Jo relished having him on the disabled list.

They hadn't solved a damned thing, but Quinn had advised him to be patient. By going after the wood he'd robbed her of all control. Nobody liked that. Also, she was a logical thinker and what he could do regarding animals wasn't logical to her.

Getting the wood had been the right thing to do. Could he have handled it better? Maybe. She could have handled it better, too. Neither of them deserved a relationship trophy this weekend.

Quinn thought they still had a shot. Brendan wasn't sure, but being allowed to make love to her was like money in the bank. It couldn't hurt and it just might help.

She brought in another towel from the bathroom along with the kettle of what used to be hot water. Too hot, in fact. When he'd touched the steamy washcloth to his donger he'd yelped and automatically jerked his head up, hitting it on the corner of the vanity.

"Sit on the towel so I can check your wound."

He sat cross-legged and managed to keep the bath towel in place.

"Okay, take the hand towel away." She knelt beside him with a damp washcloth. "Wow, you really did smear blood everywhere, didn't you?"

"Panicked. Couldn't see where it was coming from."

"Neither can I." Rising up on her knees, she began dabbing at his forehead. "Let me know if I'm hurting you."

"Like I said, it doesn't hurt much at all." Her breasts, covered up with clothes, were very close to his cheek. If he turned his head, he could kiss the swell of them under the material of her t-shirt and bra. She'd taken off the sweatshirt now that she was right next to the fire.

"I'm glad you're not in pain, but I'd like to find out where—ah, there's the gusher, just above your hairline. Abrasions to the face and head always bleed like crazy."

"Sounds like you have experience." He enjoyed the rise and fall of her breasts as she breathed. The pace increased the longer she was close to him, gently cleaning up the blood.

"I'm the mother of a tomboy and the honorary aunt of Kendra's five rambunctious boys."

"Accidents?"

"All the time, but nothing very serious, thank God." She put down the washcloth and picked up a tube of ointment. "This might sting a little."

It did and he winced.

"Sorry."

"No worries."

"It's stopped bleeding, so I'm not going to bandage it, after all. Your hair's so thick the bandage would just get stuck in it. Unless you want me to shave that part of your head."

"Hell, no. Then everybody'll be askin' what I did to myself."

"And you'd rather not say?" She sounded amused.

"You've got that right. Am I good to go, then?"

She sat back on her heels and gazed at him. "Depends on what you have in mind."

"A sponge bath."

"Want some help?"

"Definitely." He waggled his eyebrows and discovered that hurt. "Ouch."

"I'll refill the kettle and warm it over the fire." She stood and picked it up.

"What should I do?"

"Relax. And ditch the towel."

"Only if you'll ditch your clothes, too."

"But I don't need a sponge bath." Her voice was light and teasing as she turned on the kitchen faucet.

"You will when I get through with you. I'm in the mood to get hot and sweaty."

"Then taking a sponge bath first makes no sense."

"Good point. Let's wait." His heart lifted. They could leave the serious stuff alone for now and just—

"Brendan! The light just came on over the stove!"

He turned to look. "What do you know? That's great." Funny, but having power restored wasn't the thrill he would have expected.

"I can heat water on the stove."

"Yea, yea, you can." He stood and secured the towel around his hips. He'd get nudie when she did. "Was kinda fun heating it over the fire, though."

"It was. I guess it would be silly to keep doing it now that the stove's working."

"Definitely more trouble. On the other hand—" His phone chimed from the bathroom counter where he'd left it. "I'll get that. Probably Andy or Seth." He strode quickly down the hall and grabbed the phone before it went to voicemail. Seth's number was on the screen. "Hey, mate."

"Power's back on, dude! I can start on your truck, probably have it done sometime early tonight. Highways are getting clear, too. How's the buffalo situation?"

"Still out there."

"Fingers crossed they'll be gone in the morning. In past years, they usually headed out when the weather changed. We have a warming trend, so I predict they'll be on the move tonight."

"That would be terrific."

"Let me know. I'll have your vehicle ready to roll. How long was the resort reservation for?"

"Through Monday mornin'."

"Then maybe you'll get to enjoy one night there, at least, so you and Jo can soak up a little luxury before you head home."

"Maybe so." He should add that he hoped the herd would take off tonight. But that would be a lie. He liked having them out there, and if they stayed, he and Jo could, too. He wasn't sure what would happen once they were free to leave. Jo might call it quits.

He carried his phone back into the living room and set it on the table. Out of habit he plugged it into the mobile charger.

"You can use a wall socket, now," Jo said. "There's one here in the kitchen above the counter. That's what I used."

"Right." He carried the phone and power cord over there. After plugging his cord in and laying his phone next to hers, he glanced around. "The stove light's out."

"I turned it off. We don't need light now."

"True. Where'd you put the kettle?"

"I hung it over the fire."

He grinned. "You did?"

"Yeah." She came closer and slid her arms around his neck. "Heating water on the stove is boring."

"Exactly what I was thinkin'." He bracketed her hips and pulled her close. "Seth estimates he'll have my truck ready in a few hours. Historically the buffalo herd moves out when the weather changes." He held her gaze. "If they leave tonight, which is likely, and the highways are clear, we can leave in the mornin'."

"I see." Her expression was hard to read.

"Thought you should know."

"I appreciate the info. Then you're saying this could be our last night in this cabin."

"Yes, ma'am."

"What shall we do to commemorate that?"

"I vote for hauling all the bedding back over to the fire and gettin' nudie." He hesitated. "But I'll leave that decision to you."

Her smile was beautiful to behold. "I think that's a wonderful idea."

"Thank you." Lowering his head, he slowly took possession of her mouth. The pleasure of touching her soft lips made him dizzy with gratitude. When she'd delivered her ultimatum, he'd had no idea if he'd ever get to kiss her again.

Or have her kiss him back. And did she ever. With a low moan, she cupped his head and pulled him down into paradise. Her supple mouth teased him with the flavor of mint tea, the heat of dark passion and the promise of sensual delights.

He delved deep with his tongue as she snuggled against him, her breasts cushioning his pecs, her hips cradling his needy cock. She kissed with her whole being, and the gift of surrender she offered drove him crazy. Had since the first time in the back seat of his truck.

Kissing her was almost enough. Almost. He pulled back, gasping. "We're not...we don't have..."

She wiggled out of his grasp. "Get the blankets and the condoms. I'll meet you by the fireplace." Her gaze lowered. "You and your eager friend."

Sometime during the kiss he'd lost the towel. His uncovered cock stood proud and oh, so ready. He grinned. "We'll both be there."

Crossing to the bed, he scooped up the blankets and grabbed the condoms from the chair sitting next to it. Didn't take him long at all, but by the time he headed back toward the fireplace, she was nudie.

She stood facing him, the fire behind her and a welcoming smile on her kiss-reddened lips. His breath caught and he paused to drink in the sight of her. What if this was the last...no, wipe out that negative thought.

"You okay?"

"Couldn't be better." He hurried over, tossed the box of condoms to one side and dropped the blankets in a heap between them. "We need to—"

"Let me." She stooped down, clutched a section of the jumbled bedding in each hand and shook hard. The blankets billowed up, settled and lay reasonably flat.

"You're magic."

"I know." She stretched out on her side and patted a spot next to her. "Bring all that manly beauty down here, please."

"Glad to oblige." He mirrored her, lying on his side, his head propped on his hand. "Just lookin' at you makes me happy."

Her eyes sparkled. "We could just lie here quietly and admire each other, then."

"Nah." He scooted closer. "I wanna get hot and sweaty." Cradling her cheek, he brushed his lips over hers. "Judgin' from the way you reacted a little while ago, you might like that, too."

"Could be."

"Let's find out." He gave her an open-mouthed kiss as he gently fondled her silken breast. He'd take his time, savor every moment of the journey…

Then she wrapped her warm fingers around his cock and squeezed.

He eased back from the kiss. "Tryin' to tell me somethin'?"

"I am."

"What?"

"Let's get this show on the road."

That made him smile. "Not movin' fast enough for you?"

"Remember that short fuse you mentioned a while ago?"

"I do."

"It's even shorter, now."

He laughed. "Alrighty, then. Where'd I put that box of—"

"Right here." She let go of him, reached over her head and plopped the box between them.

That made him laugh even harder. He sat up and opened it. "You're somethin' else, Jo Fielding. Do you want to put it on for me, too?"

"No, thanks. I like watching you do it. Turns me on."

"Doesn't sound like you need any more turnin' on." He ripped open a packet and rolled on the condom.

"Am I too much for you?"

"God, no. I love it. Now lie back, you hot woman. I'm comin' in." Moving between her thighs, he entered her with one firm thrust. "How's that?"

She gazed up at him, her eyes luminous. "It's great." She drew in a ragged breath. "Really, really great."

"I know." *Please don't throw it away.*

26

Perfect. Jo had never experienced perfect while making love...until Brendan. Foreplay was all well and good and climaxes were wonderful, but this was what she craved—a connection like no other, as if she and Brendan were two parts of a whole.

Were they made for each other? She was trying hard to deny it, but the evidence was mounting. It was there in his eyes as he loved her with long, sure strokes. It was there in her body's joyful response.

She wrapped him in her arms as delicious tension swirled in her core. She was edging closer to a climax and she didn't want one. Not yet.

As if he'd sensed that, he eased up the pace and leaned down, his warm breath caressing her ear. "I could do this forever."

"Me, too."

"Then let's make it last." Lifting his head, he held her gaze as he settled into a lazy rhythm.

Mesmerizing. She floated in a sea of pleasure, drifting closer to release, then riding a slow current away again as he paused, dragged in air and began again.

Dusk approached, cloaking the cabin in shadows, increasing the intimacy, as if they were the only two people in the world. Firelight sparkled in his eyes and reflected off the sheen of moisture on his muscled shoulders.

He pushed deep and held very still. "I don't want to come." His voice was low, sensual. "But I'm—"

"I'm close." A slight tremor made her gasp.

"Felt that." He groaned. "I need…"

"Me, too…ahh, Brendan…*Brendan.* Without warning, her climax surged through her, arching her body like a drawn bow. The raw power of it wrenched incoherent cries from her throat until she was hoarse and panting.

With a roar, Brendan followed her, his body wracked with convulsions as he braced himself above her and gulped for air.

Gripping his taut biceps, she sank back to the floor and struggled to breathe.

"Dear God." His expression was dazed. "I've never…come…like that." He peered at her. "Are you okay?"

She wasn't up to forming words so she nodded, instead.

"I loved it. But wow."

She swallowed. "Wow…is right."

"You're sure you're okay?"

"More than okay." She took a shaky breath. "That was incredible."

"Not too much?"

"Are you kidding?" She smiled. "It was glorious."

He gave a whoop of delight. "That's what I like to hear. Listen, don't go away. I have to take the condom walk, but after that we can see about our sponge baths."

"I won't go away. I'm not sure I can move at all."

"Did I break you?"

"I'm not broken. Just boneless. If you picked me up, I'd flop around like a ragdoll."

"Then it looks like I'll be spongin' you." He kissed her lightly on the mouth. "Be back soon."

His energy amazed her. Maybe Kendra was right and he was some kind of superman. He'd left the room with a purposeful stride and in a few minutes his steps were equally brisk as he came back down the hall.

He stepped into the firelight and laid folded towels and washcloths on top of the blankets. "I want to check on something." He straightened and walked across the room to the window.

Despite her lethargy, she managed to prop herself up on her elbow. "What do you see?"

"The sky's clear and the stars are out. There's a slice of moon."

"What else?"

He turned toward her. "The buffalo are gone."

"You're kidding."

"No, ma'am."

"Maybe they're all around in front or the other side of the house."

"Good point. I'll go look."

"Like that?"

"I'll put on my coat and my boots."

"That's not enough! You'll freeze your donger."

"Not if I make it quick."

"You're insane."

"So you've said."

"Brendan, for pity's sake."

"I need to know." The rustle of fabric indicated he was putting on his coat. A couple of thumps by the door meant he'd pulled his boots on.

The door creaked open and cold air blew in until he stepped outside and closed it.

Shivering, she rolled up in the top blanket and lay there staring into the darkness. What if some of the buffalo had climbed onto the porch and he was pinned against the door?

The door creaked again and he came back in. "They're gone." He sounded…sad.

"Do you wish they'd stayed?"

Silence.

"Brendan?"

"Yea, yea, I wish they'd stayed, but that would be selfish. They left because that was the right move for them. They did what they needed to."

"But you enjoyed having them around." The concept was completely foreign to her. She'd been afraid of them, but clearly he hadn't been. At least not much.

"I do wish they'd stayed." His boots thunked on the wood floor as he took them off. Then he walked into the firelight as he unbuttoned his coat. He took it off and left it on the chair. "They were fascinatin'.

"Terrifying."

"They could be if you got crossways with them. That's part of what makes them fascinatin'."

Oh, boy. She'd do well to remember that he found fearsome beasts fascinating.

He walked around the blanket bed and picked up the gloves he'd left hanging on the edge of the woodbin. He unhooked the cast iron kettle full of water and set it on the hearth. "But mainly I was hopin' they'd stay because then we couldn't leave."

"I get that. They scared me, but...it wasn't all bad."

"No." He came and sat beside her on the blanket bed. "And despite just havin' the most outstanding sexual experience of my life—"

"Mine, too."

"I'm glad for that, but I can't shake the feelin' that once we drive away from here, that's the end." He glanced at her. "Am I wrong?"

"No."

"Listen, Jo, we—"

"We have totally different approaches to life. Just now when you blithely walked out on the porch, I wondered if you'd get pinned against the door by buffalo that had climbed up there."

"None of that happened."

"But it could have. I don't want to fall in love with someone who is destined to be mangled, crushed, or eaten before he reaches a ripe old age."

"Then you're not in love with me, yet?"

She stared at him as the horrible truth dawned. Yes, she was, damn it. But if she told him, that would make everything a thousand times worse. "No, I'm not. Dodged that bullet."

"Lucky you." He glanced away. "Ready for a sponge bath?"

"You go ahead. I don't—"

"I've been lookin' forward to givin' you one." He reached for one of the towels next to him and spread it out. "Roll onto that and I'll take care of the rest."

"You don't have to do that."

"Indulge me. If we're callin' it quits tomorrow, let me get my thrills while I can."

"If you think a sponge bath will lead to something, I have to warn you I'm wiped out."

"I don't expect it to lead to anythin'. It will give me pleasure to make you feel good. I can't speak for you, but after that last go-round, I'm sticky."

She smiled. Couldn't help it. "You're the most charming man I've ever met. I wish we could—"

"So do I. And here's the thing. I'm not goin' anywhere. I'll be in Eagles Nest for the duration. Who knows? Maybe in a year or two, you'll change your mind."

"In a year or two you'll have found the one you were meant to be with."

He held her gaze. "I don't think so. Now roll over onto this towel and let me get to work."

She was too tired to protest, so she did as he asked. The warm washcloth felt heavenly. And soothing. There was nothing sexual about his ministrations. But there was a hell of a lot of caring involved. Didn't take a genius to figure out why. He'd fallen for her, too.

After he cleaned her up, he dried her off and wrapped her in the blankets. She tried to stay awake. She really did. It was their last night and he likely wanted to make love at least once more. But she lost the fight.

When she woke up, the fire was nearly out and gray light seeped in the window. It was morning. Brendan lay beside her, eyes closed, chest rising and falling in a steady rhythm.

Oh, yeah, she loved him. But he was not for her. Someday he'd find another daredevil and they'd have great adventures together. He wouldn't be happy with someone who winced every time he proposed some new and reckless plan.

She slipped away without waking him and put on her clothes. Then she heated water on the stove and made tea. A rinsed bowl sat on the side of the sink. He must have finished off the leftover veggie stew after she'd conked out.

By the time the tea had steeped, he was awake and sitting up.

She walked over by the fire. "Good morning."

"Good morning to you." He scrubbed a hand over his face. "Feel like I've been rode hard and put away wet."

"I'm not surprised. You held out longer than I did."

"Not much longer. I gave myself a quick bath, ate some stew and crawled under the covers.

Got up once to beef up the fire. I should probably do that again."

"Or not. No point in building it up if we'll be leaving soon."

"True."

"If we text Ida, she'd probably feed us breakfast before we leave."

"Much as I hate to impose, that idea makes my mouth water."

"Mine, too. I'd pay her generously, but she probably won't take it."

"I was thinkin' about their situation while I was eatin' the stew. I need to invest in somethin' anyway, so I'd like to invest in their business." He glanced at her. "That's assumin' you're serious about givin' them some pointers. They need help."

"I'm serious. But I think we should come clean about our relationship if we're going to be dealing with them professionally. We can't keep pretending that—"

"Yea, yea, you're absolutely right." He threw back the covers and stood. "Let's do this thing."

Good Lord, he was beautiful. She ought to look away, but this was the last time she'd see him nudie. She sighed and met his amused gaze. "Forgive me. I was ogling."

"Now see there? That gives me a smidgen of hope."

"But I'm not—"

"Yea, yea, you're not in the market. But if you ever are, I'll be easy to find."

27

Working with his Goondeen had taught Brendan quite a bit about restraint. He used every bit of that training as he progressed through a sucky morning that would end with saying goodbye to Jo.

It wouldn't mean he'd never see her again. She had his money in her bank, for one thing. And his older brother spent most of his time with Jo's best friend. Eagles Nest was a small town and he intended to be a part of the community. Their paths would cross.

But she'd made it clear that she didn't want to continue what they'd started, and that hurt like a sonofabitch.

Seth drove up to fetch them in Brendan's truck. The front grill looked like hell, but Seth promised the truck would run fine. He hopped in the back seat while Brendan drove them back. Sure enough, the truck seemed okay.

Their arrival at the main house started off rocky as he and Jo confessed to Ida that they weren't married. She was gracious about it, all things considered, and insisted on feeding them breakfast anyway. She was somewhat mollified when Jo set up an appointment to help her create a business plan and he offered an infusion of cash.

He longed to tell Ida that if Jo would have him, he'd marry her in a minute, but saying that wouldn't be fair to Jo, like it was her fault they weren't hitched. Which it was, but he wouldn't place blame like that. You didn't do such a thing to someone you loved.

And he loved Jo Fielding. He thought she might love him, too, even if she'd lied and said she didn't. He forgave her that lie. She likely thought telling him would make it worse. It might have.

After breakfast and a long goodbye filled with hugs, handshakes and backslaps, he helped Jo into the passenger seat of the truck and started up the bumpy road to the highway.

She settled back in her seat. "That wasn't too bad."

"Which part?" If *not too bad* was her evaluation of the entire episode, they had an argument coming.

"Admitting to Ida that we aren't married."

"Yea, yea, she took it better'n I expected."

"I was surprised when she insisted I take some of her canned goods home and wouldn't let me pay for them."

"She just plain likes you. I don't think you fit her image of a fallen woman."

"Just like you don't fit her image of a wicked man."

"Oh, I'm wicked all right."

"I suppose you are, at that."

He glanced over and she had a cute little smile on her face. All was not lost.

Reaching down, she plucked something from the floor and held it up. "French fry."

"Seth must've missed it when he cleaned out the cab." He winked at her. "Are you goin' to eat it?"

"I should, just to gross you out."

"Don't."

"I won't, but now that I've picked it up, I can't put it back on the floor where guaranteed I'll step on it and grind it into your floor mat."

"Now there's a major issue. I'll have you know this is a brand-new truck. Heaven forbid the floor mat gets dirty."

"I know, right? Desiree would hate that."

"You remembered her name." Another good sign.

"How could I forget? It's not often you meet a truck named Desiree."

"That's for sure." He pulled over to the side of the road and unfastened his seat belt. "Let me have the fry. Some critter will love it." He took it from her, stepped down carefully on the frozen ground and located a rock protruding from the snow. He laid the fry there and climbed back behind the wheel.

"That was very nice of you."

"Wasn't doin' us any good in here."

"You could have tossed it in the snow somewhere."

"Wanted somethin' to be able to find it."

"I know."

The way she was looking at him made him consider a kiss. Was there hope, after all? "I guess we could still head to the resort for one night. We didn't exactly decide what comes next."

"I have." She said it quietly, without smiling. "I apologize if I left you hanging."

"No worries." He hadn't wanted to ask any earlier and have her confirm what he suspected.

She took a deep breath. "The past two days have been...like a high-speed rollercoaster. I'll never forget this experience, but I'm...I'm ready to get off the ride." Her gaze was troubled, as if she didn't like making that speech any more than he liked hearing it.

He swallowed. "Okay." Snapping his seat belt into place, he pulled back on the road. Not much to say after that. Music? Nope. Not the time for it.

A winter sun shone on the highway, melting the last of the ice on the edges of the asphalt. Not many folks were on the road this Sunday morning. Driving back to Eagles Nest would be a breeze.

Except the silence ate at him, partly because he could hear Jo breathing. The sound made him ache all over.

"Seth did a great job with the truck," he said at last, desperate to distract himself. "I wish he would've taken more for the repair."

She picked up her cue, thank God. "That's something I'll talk to Ida about during our meeting. They're generous to a fault, but if they don't start charging what their goods and services are worth, they'll continue to struggle."

"I'll need your advice on how much to invest with them. I was vague on the amount 'cause I wanted to discuss it with you, first." Good. They were talking, even if it was about something mundane like investing his money. Anything was better than that horrible silence, as if they were two strangers riding down the road.

"You should have more than one investment. I recommend a portfolio. I have a broker in Bozeman if you—"

"I'll stick with your recommendations for now." *Forever.* His savings had never been a strong focus, but the money had given him an excuse to contact her in the beginning. He'd continue to use that excuse. "How did you get into banking in the first place?"

"I loved math in school. I worked my way through college with my job as a bank teller and I liked it so much I decided not to become an accountant, after all. I'm glad. The Eagles Nest Bank is perfect for me."

"I like that old buildin'. It has character."

"Isn't it great? I love working there. The maintenance crew uses lemon oil on the wood, which makes it smell terrific. Ida uses lemon oil, too."

"Noticed that."

"She's a born hostess. And the cabin is a little rough, but it has character, too."

"Yep." His favorite cabin in the whole world.

"Whatever you invest should go to fixing it up."

"I like that idea a lot. Might go out and supervise the operation. Wouldn't want them destroyin' what's special about it." Although no one could destroy his memories, which were the most special part of all.

"Exactly. Like the fireplace."

"That's why I want to supervise. I don't want anyone touchin' the fireplace."

"Maybe hire a chimney sweep, though."

"Yea, yea, maintenance is fine, so long as they don't tear it out and start over."

"Or cover up the logs with wallboard instead of filling in the chinks. Putting up wallboard and insulation would be cheaper and easier, but it would change the whole feel of being there."

"Definitely. If I'm an investor, I can have some say in it." He'd mentioned to Andy that if they decided to rent the cabin again, they might want to block out February to give the buffalo a chance to come and go. Andy had agreed.

"I'll talk to Kendra about how they renovated their historic cabin. I'm sure she has some suggestions and tips for filling in the space between the logs. Have you seen that little place?"

"Just from the outside. I'll ask to check it out, take pictures." He looked over at her. "Are you sayin' you'd like to be part of this renovation project?"

She hesitated. "Well, no, probably not. I'll leave that to you."

He kicked himself for opening his mouth. He'd startled her and yanked her out of the fantasy. She'd been back there, picturing the place and wanting to preserve and protect it, just as he had. *Way to shut down the lines of communication, bozo.*

She pulled out her phone. "I need to text Mandy and let her know I'll be home a day early. Kendra, too."

"If you'd ask Kendra to tell Quinn, I'd appreciate it."

"That's right, you're still living there." Her fingers moved rapidly over the screen. "How's that working out?"

"Fine for now. Kendra's friend Deidre is all set to find me a place to buy when I'm ready. That'll take some of the money I handed to you."

"Have you ever owned property?"

"No, ma'am. It's my first time for that, too."

"*Too*? What else?"

Slip of the tongue. "Investin' in someone's business. Never have done that before." Wasn't what he'd been referring to, though. Turned out he'd fallen madly, deeply in love for the very first time in his life.

<u>28</u>

Stay strong. Jo repeated the mantra over and over as Brendan pulled his truck into a visitor parking space in her condo complex parking lot. He was hurting. She hated that.

But he couldn't change who he was and she wouldn't ask or expect him to. She had the buffalo to thank for disclosing his true nature. Without that experience, she'd have been oblivious to his daredevil streak.

No wonder he was such an exciting lover. He liked living on the edge. She liked living somewhere in the middle.

He was out of the truck before she'd unfastened her seat belt. After helping her down, where touching couldn't be avoided, he pulled her suitcase out of the backseat. "I'll take this up for you."

"Please don't."

"No worries. I won't pester you about comin' in. But I'm not droppin' you off and lettin' you haul your luggage in by yourself." He picked it up and started off.

"Do you know where you're going?"

He paused, a sheepish expression on his handsome face. "Not exactly."

"It's the other direction." She led him along a shoveled pathway that wound through evergreen shrubs dusted with snow.

"Maintenance crew does a nice job."

"That's one of the reasons I live here. Being next to Wild Creek Ranch and Kendra was great, but the house and yard were a burden. I don't have to shovel snow or pull weeds."

"Whereas I can't wait to have my own place so I can do those things. Never had four walls I could do whatever I wanted with. Haven't had my own horse since I left for 'stralia."

"Then you'll be looking for a place outside town?"

"Yes, ma'am. I might try and talk Quinn into sellin' me some acreage. He's added onto his parcel and he's admitted he doesn't have plans for it, yet."

"That sounds nice for both of you."

"Yea, yea, we could turn it into the Sawyer compound. Kendra's all for it. That lady's big on family togetherness."

"So am I."

"Then we'll be seein' a lot of each other."

Yikes. "Yes. Yes, we will." Hadn't parsed that out, had she? In her role as Aunt Jo, she attended every McGavin celebration. Now the Sawyers were invited, too. Including Uncle Brendan.

She paused by her front door. "We're here."

"Ah." He put down her suitcase and gazed at her. "I honestly hadn't thought of that, either."

"What?"

"That we'd be seein' each other all the time at family functions. With people gettin' married and kids bein' born, not to mention holidays, birthdays and such, we'll have somethin' goin' on—"

"Nearly every weekend."

"That's about the size of it." He picked up his hat and settled it at a slightly different, more rakish angle. "You okay with that?"

Dear God, she *was*, and there was the problem. She wanted to gobble him up right this minute, even if he was the worst choice in the world. How would she handle seeing his tempting self on a regular basis?

She blew out a breath. "It is what it is."

He nodded. "That's a fact." But he didn't look as dejected as he had earlier. A thoughtful gleam had replaced the misery in his gray eyes. "Be seein' you, Jo." Touching two fingers to the brim of his hat, he sauntered off.

He should have a license for that sexy, loose-hipped walk. She fought the urge to call him back, to invite him in, to...oh, yeah, all of that.

At the end of the path he turned, glanced over his shoulder and caught her staring. He grinned, the rat. Lifting his hat in salute, he rounded the corner and was gone.

But not forgotten. Not that she ever could, but thanks to the family connection, she'd have absolutely no opportunity to forget Brendan Sawyer. She was in for it.

* * *

From the moment Kendra called to announce a meeting of the Whine and Cheese Club the following Friday night, Jo suspected a trap, or at the very least ulterior motives. She'd texted everyone early in the week to say she was home and they'd responded by welcoming her back.

After that they'd gone silent. Or if they were communicating, it wasn't with her. Now Kendra was calling a meeting. Something was up.

"If this is some grand scheme to change my mind about Brendan, I'm not coming."

"It's just movie night," Kendra said. "We all got busy after the holidays and we haven't had movie night in ages. Everyone's bringing jammies."

"And it's just us, right? No kids. No grandkids."

"Just us. Quinn's staying over at his house."

"What about Brendan?"

"I thought you didn't want to talk about him."

"I don't. I just want to be sure he won't pop out at the appropriate moment."

"When would that be?"

"After you've brainwashed me."

"I promise on the Sacred Ouija Board that Brendan will be nowhere near my house tonight. Come over. Bring wine and whatever food you have on hand."

"Okay. What are we watching?"

"Deidre's bringing her stash. We'll have lots of choices."

"I vote for *Murder on the Orient Express.*"

"Duly noted. See you at six."

She arrived right on time and everyone else's vehicle was already parked in front of the ranch house. Wood smoke drifted from the chimney and laughter spilled from the house, even with the doors and windows closed.

She smiled. They were a rambunctious group and because of them, she'd become more rambunctious, too, especially after divorcing Robert. He'd never approved of the Whine and Cheese Club.

Carrying her bag of goodies in one hand and an overnight bag in the other, she walked in without knocking. After leaving her coat on the rack by the door, she took her stuff over by the coffee table where everyone was having a loud discussion about which movie to watch. Her choice lay there along with *Pretty Woman, The Princess Bride, Dirty Dancing, Beaches, Crocodile Dundee*...aha!

She put down her bags and snatched it up. "How long were you all going to debate before everyone except me voted for this one?"

Deidre, her hair in a Lucille Ball up-do, batted her eyelashes in a great imitation of Lucy. "Honey, we wouldn't dream of watching that if you don't want to."

"Well, I don't. Anything but that."

"Great." Christine, the only blond in the group, dug in her overnight bag. "Because I just got this and I'm dying to see it. I missed it in the theater and I never seem to catch it on TV, either." She held up *The Legend of Tarzan.*

"Cool! I'll open it." Judy's ponytail bobbed as she took the DVD. "I'm good at freeing these puppies from their shrink wrap."

"I love me some Alexander Skarsgard." Kendra glanced at Jo. "How about you?"

"Yes." Jo drilled her with a look. "You know I do. We went to see that together." She turned to Christine. "Exactly when did you order this?"

"Oh, I don't know. Recently."

"How recently?"

Christine sighed, got up from the floor and came over to hug Jo. "I cannot tell a lie. I ordered it day before yesterday and put a rush on it because we all agreed that this was the one you needed to watch. I haven't seen it, but I looked at the trailers and I totally agree this is a must for you."

"But I've already—"

"That's not the point." Kendra slung an arm around her shoulders. "Timing is everything. You need to see it again."

"So this is a setup, after all."

"No, honey." Deidre moved in to join the group hug. "It's more like an intervention."

"You guys weren't there. You can't imagine how reckless he was, how careless about his own safety. I can't—"

"Just watch the movie." Judy gazed at her with affection. "Ever since Robert, you've been...jaded."

"No, I've been realistic."

"Jaded," Deidre said. "You don't believe in heroes anymore. And that's a crying shame, because they still exist."

"Not like in the movies!"

"Exactly like in the movies," Christine said. "They show up in the news all the time. Some are ordinary guys and some are extraordinary. We trust Quinn and he's convinced us his brother falls in the extraordinary category."

"But I don't want a hero!"

"Are you sure you don't?" Kendra gave her shoulder a squeeze. "You're still wearing the ring he gave you."

"You are?" Deidre grabbed Jo's left hand. "I'll be damned. I didn't notice in all the hubbub. Why didn't you give it back?"

"I forgot when he dropped me off at the condo. Then I left it on so I'd give it back the next time I saw him. I was afraid if I took it off, I'd lose it, and—"

"Uh-huh." Deidre examined the ring. "And if you believe that, I have a bridge I'd like to sell you. You want this hero, whether you know it or not."

"I don't either. Heroes are scary."

"And noble and amazing," Deidre said. "Watch the movie. See if you recognize any of Tarzan's behavior."

Judy clasped her hands together. "Please, Jo. Watch it. Do it for us, if nothing else. We love you and after Robert you deserve someone special. Don't settle for ordinary. Go for the hero."

"Okay, okay. I'll watch it." She handed her bag of goodies to Kendra and picked up her overnight bag. "While you're queuing it up I'll put on my jammies." She started down the hall to the guest bathroom.

"We'll pour you some wine," Kendra called after her.

"Make it a very big glass!" She changed quickly and left her clothes where everyone else had dumped theirs—in one of the boys' old rooms. They did love her and she'd be an ungrateful woman if she didn't appreciate their effort to help. It wouldn't change anything, but she'd watch the damn movie.

An hour and fifty minutes later, she was in tears and her friends were dispensing hugs, more wine and tissues.

Kendra peered at her. "Are those happy tears or sad tears?"

"I don't know," she wailed. "Maybe both!"

"Meltdowns are good." Deidre patted her on the back. "They come from facing our fears."

"That's for sure." Jo blew her nose. "I'm scared shitless. I'm in love with a hero. What am I supposed to do about that?"

"You could woman up and tell him," Christine said. "Or you can chicken out. Your choice."

"And that's tough love right there, honey." Deidre handed her a fresh glass of wine. "Want this for some Dutch courage?"

She gazed at the wine. "No. I've had enough wine." She got to her feet and was relieved to discover that she was only slightly drunk. "I'm gonna tell him, and I'd like to tell him tonight, but going over to Quinn's house to see him doesn't appeal to me and I probably shouldn't drive, anyway." She turned to Kendra. "Did you stash him somewhere, after all?"

Laughter danced in Kendra's green eyes. "Yeah, I did."

"I knew it! Is he hiding back in your bedroom? Because I don't want to tell him in front of you guys, either. This should be a private—"

"He's in the cabin."

She stared at her best friend. "Then I'm outta here." She headed for the coatrack.

"Wait, wait," Kendra hurried after her. "You need something on your feet."

"I'll get her boots." Christine ran down the hall.

"I guess boots would be good." She pulled on her black coat over her jammies and allowed Christine to help her on with her boots. "See you guys later." As she opened the door, her friends started cheering and whistling.

They kept it up even after she closed the door and stood on the porch. She sucked in a lungful of frigid air. Her hero was waiting.

29

Brendan was a man of action. Waiting to see if watching a movie would change Jo's mind was his version of hell. But Quinn had advised him to go along with it. His big brother put faith in the Whine and Cheese Club.

He passed some time examining the chinking material between the cabin's ancient logs. He took pictures with his phone so he'd have something to show the Culbertsons. That used fifteen, maybe twenty minutes.

Kendra had texted him after Jo had arrived and he'd driven over and hiked up to the cabin then, just in case. No telling when someone would spill the beans that he was there and Jo would take a notion to come up.

Or not. If she found out he was there and chose not to show, Kendra had promised to let him know so he could drive back home. But he concentrated on the image of her making the climb up the hill and knocking on the cabin door, even if all she did was chew him out for taking part in such a cockamamie scheme.

The movie was an hour and fifty minutes long. He paced and checked his watch. He'd built a small fire for atmosphere. Unlike the cabin last weekend, this one had all the amenities, so the fire wasn't a necessity.

Kinda took the fun out of building one, too. He'd relished the challenge of depending on the fireplace as the only heat source. The buffalo herd had added another layer of adventure—for him, anyway. Jo had reacted quite differently.

How the hell could a movie about Tarzan make her rethink her position? He'd never lived in the jungle. He couldn't swing from trees and he'd never learned to yell like that, either. He didn't get it, but Quinn said Kendra and the others knew what they were doing.

Eventually he needed fresh air, so he went out on the porch. He kept poking his head back in the door to check the fire, but it was a tiny fire compared to what he'd been creating in the other cabin. Now that had been a fire to remember.

Damn, this was a long-ass time to wait. His Goondeen would tell him it was good for his spiritual growth. Okay, he'd treat it that way. He went back in the cabin and sat quietly staring into the fire. Used up a few more minutes before he had to head for the porch again for a while.

He kept up that routine until one time he walked out on the porch and saw her come out the door of the ranch house. Hot damn. He took the steps two at a time. "Jo!"

She looked up, saw him and started running.

"Be careful!"

"Don't wanna!" She slipped on some ice in the parking area but regained her balance.

"Slow down!" He started running, too, but it was harder going downhill. "You'll hurt yourself!"

"I don't care!"

"Well, I do! I love you!"

"I love you, too!"

Holy hell. She loved him. And she was saying it out loud. He put on a burst of speed and got to the bottom of the hill at the same moment she reached it.

He swung her up in his arms. "I love you, I love you, I love you!"

"I love you, too!" She was panting, sending clouds of vapor into the air. "Where's your coat?"

"I—" He started to laugh. "I forgot it."

"You left it at home?"

"It's in the cabin."

"Aren't you cold?"

"How could I be?" He pulled her close and lowered his head until his lips almost touched hers. "You're here." Then he kissed her. Funniest thing, but he could swear he heard people cheering.

Epilogue

"Aleck, I need to borrow money for a plane ticket to America." Rory McGavin walked into his older brother's law office unannounced. "Once I'm there I'll get a job so I can pay—"

"Whoa, whoa." Aleck pushed back his desk chair and stood. "What's goin' on? Why are you—"

"I'm in a wee bit of a guddle. Need to leave Scotland tonight."

"Is someone after you?"

"Aye, they will be."

His brother's eyes widened. "What the hell did you do?"

"Slept with the boss's daughter."

Aleck groaned. "Only you, Rory."

"She seduced me, I tell you! I tried to resist, but she's a bonnie lass and she's been flirtin' with me for weeks."

"Then what's the problem?"

"Turns out she's a virgin. Or was until last night. Needless to say, I didn't know in advance or I would have bowed out."

"Understood, but I still don't know why you're set on leavin'."

"She expects me to marry her. Evidently she's had her eye on me from my first day at the distillery. Said I reminded her of Prince Harry."

"You don't look anythin' like Prince Harry."

"It's the hair. She's into gingers."

"Then she can find herself another one."

"She says it has to be me. She promised her da that she'd save herself for the man she chose to marry. She can't imagine why I'm not thrilled with the idea of sharin' her life and eventual inheritance."

"So her little scheme didn't work. So what? This is the twenty-first century. Nobody's comin' after you with a shotgun."

"I wouldn't be too sure about that. She said if I don't do the right thing, her da will see that I never work in the distillery industry again and her brothers will likely ambush me in a dark alley."

"Hey, that's blackmail. Get her threats on tape and we'll take her to court."

"Thanks for the support, but the plain truth is, I should've known better. If I quietly disappear, she'll likely forget about me and move on to some other Prince Harry lookalike. I don't have the necessary funds, but if you'll advance me the—"

"I'd rather take her to court." Aleck sighed. "But if you insist on bein' a gentleman, I'll book you a ticket." He called up a site on his computer. "America's a large target. Got a particular destination in mind?"

"Bozeman, Montana."

Aleck looked up. "Montana? Isn't that where—"

"Aye. Thought I'd visit our long-lost cousins. Try my hand at roundin' up doggies, or whatever it is they do over there."

"Unless I'm mistaken, you've never been on a horse."

"No, but I'm in shape. How hard can it be?"

"Guess you'll find out." He turned back to his computer and tapped on the keys. "Did you contact them? Let them know you're comin'?"

"Nope. Don't want anyone to make a fuss."

Aleck gazed at him. "Or ask too many questions about why you're suddenly flyin' across the pond?"

"That, too."

"Got you a flight out. Want to book a return?"

"Not yet. Playin' it by ear."

"Clearly. I'm adding a rental so you can get where you're goin'. Just remember they drive on the wrong side of the road."

"Thanks. Didn't think of that. Or gettin' a rental. I'll pay it all back."

"I know." His brother finalized the reservation. "You're all set. You'll have a layover in Chicago. Then you're off to the wild, wild West."

"Appreciate your help."

"No problem." Aleck shook his head and grinned. "A ginger Scottish cowboy. That's bloody hilarious. Wish I could be there."

Rory gave him an eye roll. "I'll send you pictures."

* * * * *

Rory walked with Damaris toward three saddled horses tied to the hitching post in front of the barn.

Damaris swept a hand in his direction. "Quinn, this is Rory, in case you haven't guessed."

Quinn smiled. "I have. I'm quick that way." He was holding a gray horse by the reins but he dropped them to the ground and came over to offer his hand. "Good to meet you, Rory."

"Good to meet you, too, Quinn. But aren't you worried that horse will just walk away?"

"He's ground-tied."

"What's—" He caught himself before he'd revealed his ignorance.

Even so, Quinn gave him a sharp glance.

Damaris didn't seem to notice. She'd gone over to stroke the neck of the gray horse. "Is this dappled gray for me?"

"He is. This is Fifty Shades."

She laughed. "Of course he is. Pleased to meet you, handsome guy."

"He's on loan from Crimson Cliffs Ranch. So is the palomino April's riding. We pulled from every resource we had."

"I'm thrilled with this one. The genetics that produce such a color fascinate me." She glanced at the other two. One was the color of light suede with a black mane and tail. His lower legs were black, too, as if he had on socks. "I see you have Banjo saddled. Who's the third one? I don't recognize him."

"That's Diablo. Should be perfect for you, Rory."

"I'm sure he'll be fine." Diablo? That didn't sound good. Although the brown horse didn't look much like a devil with his head drooping and his eyes closed.

"Is Diablo from Crimson Cliffs, too?" Damaris looked him over. "I don't remember a Wild Creek horse with that name."

"He's ours. Kendra and I found him a few months ago. Whoever named him has a sense of humor. Nothing devilish about this animal. He's a sound fifteen-year-old with good manners."

Some of Rory's tension eased. He was on board with a sleepy horse who had good manners. Not even Diablo's tail twitched. It wasn't braided with ribbons, likely because he hadn't been meant to ride in the wedding.

Quinn picked up the gray horse's reins and glanced at Damaris. "Ready to mount up?"

"You betcha." She approached the horse from the left, handed her bouquet to Quinn and put her booted foot in the left stirrup. Good to know that was the side to use. She mounted swiftly, despite the extra material of the split skirt. After retrieving her bouquet and riding away from the hitching post, she spun her horse around, clearly waiting for him.

He was torn. He wanted her company on the trip to the meadow, but if she stayed to watch him get on this creature, she might figure out that he'd never been astride one in his life.

IIe gazed up at her. "You'd best be goin'. Catch up with the others. I'll be right behind you."

"I can wait. We'll make Ryker's fourteen-hundred hours, no problem."

"All right." He turned toward Quinn. "Let's do it."

The light of amusement in Quinn's gray eyes said it all. He knew he was dealing with a beginner. "Then allow me to introduce you to Diablo. I think you'll like him."

"I'm sure I will."

"He may not look like it now, but having a rider on his back puts a spring in his step. He'll make you look good."

"Does he ever rear up on his hind legs?"

"Not unless you want him to." Quinn lowered his voice. "You have zero experience, right?"

Denying it was stupid. This bloke wasn't the type you could fool. "How did you know?"

"Son, I've been around riders all my life. You don't fit the profile."

"But I want to."

"That's an admirable goal. If you stay open to it, there's much to be learned on the back of a horse. Here's the deal with Diablo. He moves out as if he's in a parade, but Kendra bought him because he's great with kids."

"It's a horse for wee bairns?" Now he could breathe easy.

"I had a hunch you might not be ready for a more spirited animal. Need a boost?"

"No, thank you. I can manage." He might not know what he was doing, but he could mount up with flair, like he'd seen in the movies.

Shoving his boot in the left stirrup, he pushed off with vigor. Too much vigor, it turned out. Somehow he overshot the saddle, lost his left stirrup in the process and was forced to slide to the ground on the far side of the blasted horse. The animal turned his head and gave him a long-suffering glance. Bloody hell.

New York Times bestselling author Vicki Lewis Thompson's love affair with cowboys started with the Lone Ranger, continued through Maverick, and took a turn south of the border with Zorro. She views cowboys as the Western version of knights in shining armor, rugged men who value honor, honesty and hard work. Fortunately for her, she lives in the Arizona desert, where broad-shouldered, lean-hipped cowboys abound. Blessed with such an abundance of inspiration, she only hopes that she can do them justice.

For more information about this prolific author, visit her website and sign up for her newsletter. She loves connecting with readers.

VickiLewisThompson.com